Praise for ODD MAN OUT and Andrew Taylor

'Beautifully measured . . . Taylor's understated thriller
generates a dark, hypnotic pull' *Time Out*

'Funny, suspenseful, engagingly amoral. Splendid example
of the devil not only having the best tunes, but several top
soloists to play them.' *Literary Review*

'Andrew Taylor is a master story-teller' *Daily Telegraph*

'Taylor is, as always, adept at showing the reality beneath
the surface, as the characters interact and the unsavoury
truth behind the murder is gradually revealed'
Sunday Telegraph

'In William Dougal, Andrew Taylor has created one of the
most attractive amateur detectives in fiction' *Spectator*

'Andrew Taylor . . . was given the thumbs up long ago
for beautifully crafted, well written narratives combining
subtlety, depth and that vital "Oh, my God, what the hell
is going to happen next?" factor, which is the driving force
of the storyteller. He is also that rarity that can manage the
semi-historical as well as the modern.' *Daily Express*

'Full of nostalgic detail, this is old-fashioned crime
at its best' *The Sunday Times*

'Well-modulated, enjoyable criminous entertainment.'
Guardian

'I hope to meet the lively and amoral William Dougal again.
And again . . .' *The Times*

Also by Andrew Taylor

About the Author

Andrew Taylor is the prizewinning and bestselling author of
crime novels that include the William Dougal series,
the Lydmouth series and the ground-breaking Roth Trilogy,
as well as historical crime novels *The American Boy* and
The Anatomy of Ghosts. Andrew lives with his wife in the
Forest of Dean, on the borders of England and Wales.

To find out more, visit Andrew's website,
www.andrew-taylor.co.uk and follow him on
Twitter, twitter.com/andrewjrtaylor.

ANDREW TAYLOR

Odd Man Out

HODDER

First published in Great Britain in 1993 by Victor Gollancz Ltd

First published by Hodder & Stoughton in 2012
An Hachette UK company

2

A CIP catalogue record for this title is available
from the British Library.

Paperback ISBN 978 1 444 76572 4
Ebook ISBN 978 1 444 76573 1

Typeset in Plantin Light by Palimpsest Book Production Limited,
Falkirk, Stirlingshire

Printed and bound in the UK by Clays Ltd, St Ives plc

Hodder & Stoughton policy is to use papers that are natural,
renewable and recyclable products and made from wood grown
in sustainable forests. The logging and manufacturing processes
are expected to conform to the environmental regulations
of the country of origin.

Hodder & Stoughton Ltd
338 Euston Road
London NW1 3BH

www.hodder.co.uk

For Diane and Don

I

'Miles,' Dougal whispered. 'Come on. Get up.'

Miles Provender was lying on his stomach with his head on one side. There was something funny about a small area of his hair just above and in front of the left ear. It looked like an irregular indentation about the size of a ten-pence piece. A dark liquid gleamed among the black, wiry hairs.

'No,' Dougal said. 'Now don't be silly.'

He backed away. He stood panting by the window. It was still light outside. He had no fear of being seen. In this part of Kew one of the things you paid for was the absence of neighbours' eyes. He couldn't even see the van, which was parked a little further up the drive.

Opposite the window was a rectangle of yellow brickwork belonging to the house next door, and above the bricks was the sky. Vapour from an invisible plane made a white scratch across the blue. The house next door was empty, he remembered, because its owners were having a week of unbridled musical pleasure in Salzburg.

Sweat trickled down his back. His legs wanted to run. Sometimes a corpse affected his stomach, which was of a nervous disposition, but fortunately not in this case.

There were several telephones. The nearest one was in the kitchen. All he had to do was pick it up and dial the police.

'My name's William Dougal,' he would say. And he would give the address of the house, Celia's house. 'There's a man in one of the rooms at the back. I think he's dead.'

Dougal frowned at Miles's body. He felt as though there were a sheet of glass between them. They inhabited worlds which now ran in parallel like different television channels. In Dougal's world, Miles wasn't human, or alive, or conscious – indeed he wasn't anything other than a piece of dead meat: he had reverted to being the raw material for other forms of life. Significance had departed hand in hand with consciousness. The world – Dougal's world, that is – was not necessarily a poorer place because of it.

'I think someone killed him,' Dougal would say to the police officer.

Miles Provender was wearing jeans, a T-shirt and trainers. It was an unseasonably warm evening: perhaps he hadn't bothered to bring a jacket or a jersey, or perhaps he'd left it in his car. His arms were brown, hairy and muscular. He was in his early thirties. Once he'd played rugby football to club standard and he was still very fit. In life he had given the impression of being rather larger than he actually was. The teeth had been whiter, the smile more charming, the physical presence more arresting.

A gorgeous hunk, Dougal thought, and wondered whether some women had actually used this term about Miles without qualifying it with ironic mental quotation-marks.

On the uncarpeted floor by Miles's head was a big claw hammer. There was a red smear on the striking face. The hammer had come from the blue metal toolbox by the door. The toolbox was Celia's and was usually kept in the cupboard under the stairs. Dougal had used some of the tools, including the hammer, last night. He had needed to dismantle a bookcase and lever up some carpet tacks.

'I think someone may have hit him with a hammer,' Dougal would tell the police officer on the phone. 'Bang, bang, you're dead. His name's Miles. He's miles away now. Miles and miles and miles.'

Alone with the body in the little room at the corner of the house, Dougal began to laugh. *Miles and miles and miles.* Dead funny. No – the thing on the floor was unbelievable but not funny. Deadly serious instead. Once you started to think about it, language revealed itself as a minefield of dark, sinister humour. He shook his head from side to side and tried to think instead of Celia and Eleanor, and himself as well; he had to act for the best for all concerned. Was Miles concerned? No, because Miles was meat.

Dougal heard whispering like the rustle of dead leaves. Children said that talking to yourself was a sign of madness. His lips moved, and words spilled into the silence.

'Look after yourself because no one else will. OK, Miles? Look after Number One. You're very quiet this evening, if you don't mind my mentioning it. You look as if you're miles away. Miles and miles and miles. Get a grip on yourself.'

Miles had had a grip on something else. Dougal knelt by the body and peered at the thumb and forefinger of Miles's left hand. There was nothing there, of course, not now. A moment before they had held, pincer-like, a fragment of hashish which resembled a dried, blackened and slightly squashed pea.

'I might have known,' Miles had said.

These were the first words he had spoken that evening. Dougal had come warily into the room and there was Miles standing by the fireplace, looking pleased with himself. Dougal could have defended himself, but chose not to: he could have said that he had forgotten the hash was in the china pot on the mantel, that he hadn't touched it or even thought about it for months, if not years: and in any case what did it matter?

'That's floored you, hasn't it? I bet Celia doesn't know. Well, she soon will, and so will your employer. Jesus, it's so irresponsible, especially with a kid in the house.'

Dougal said that he thought Eleanor was a little young to smoke dope. This seemed not to reassure Miles but to upset him even more.

'I mean it, you know. This could mean a criminal record. It's not a joke.'

'I wasn't laughing,' Dougal pointed out.

'What are you doing here anyway?' Miles demanded; he was trembling, presumably with outrage. 'I thought you were moving out yesterday.'

3

'I was,' Dougal said, wishing he could sound more in charge of the situation, less on the defensive. 'I did. But it took longer than I thought it would. So I had to come back today to finish off.'

'It looks like you've hardly started.'

'You can help me load the van if you want.'

'Why should I want to do that?'

'It'll keep your hands occupied while you tell me what you're doing here.'

Miles didn't smile, he smirked. He dangled a set of house keys in front of Dougal's face. 'Celia asked me to do one or two jobs for her while she was away.'

'Here?'

'In your old room, you mean? It certainly needs it.' Miles grinned, showing the very white teeth, then licked his lips. 'Any objections?'

Dougal knew that something didn't fit. Perhaps it was simply that he didn't want it to fit. But was there an undercurrent of uncertainty beneath the surface of Miles's self-assurance?

'Why?' Dougal said softly. 'Why you?'

'Just giving a friend a helping hand.' The smirk re-emerged. 'In a manner of speaking.'

The smirk, the words and a tiny movement of Miles's right hand: ambiguous little items which Dougal added together to make a plainly monstrous total.

Miles inflated his chest. The smirk vanished. 'I don't want you bothering her any more,' he continued. 'All right? Got that?'

'Or what?'

'If you promise not to pester her, I might consider not mentioning *this*.' Miles held up the hash. 'I won't even mention seeing you. I don't want to upset her.'

Dougal considered trying to explain to Miles why his behaviour was wholly unacceptable. Celia would be the first to condemn such an unwarranted display of masculine arrogance. Dougal could also point out that each of them was an autonomous moral being, and Celia could manage her relationship with Dougal without either practical or theoretical help from Miles. Finally, in his peroration, Dougal could expand on the theme of live and let live, teaching Miles to appreciate the virtue of peaceful coexistence on this crowded planet.

Instead he felt a joyous rush of adrenalin. 'Honk, honk,' he said.

'What?'

'It's what pigs say.'

Miles's black eyebrows drew together. 'Are you mad?'

'No. I am implying not very subtly that you're a pig. Metaphorically speaking. And that's unkind to pigs.'

Dougal watched the shock spreading across Miles's face. Surprise made him look vulnerable. He wasn't used to coping with playground insults.

'Honk, honk,' Dougal said. 'Would you mind going away? Just leaving me alone while I clear out my things?'

'You little shit. I'm going to teach you a lesson.'

'Honk.'

Dougal just had time to think what a fool he had been; to feel his bravado slipping away; to feel how unseemly and squalid this business was; to feel fear. Then Miles's fist hit him in the chest, flinging him against the wall. Dougal grabbed the neck of Miles's T-shirt. Miles retaliated with a back-handed slap. Dougal staggered towards the door and tripped over the open toolbox. Miles leapt on top of him and grabbed his ears. His legs were astride Dougal's waist. Dougal screamed.

'I'm going to enjoy this,' Miles said.

Dougal's arms thrashed. His body squirmed. The fingers of his right hand touched metal and rubber. They curled round a handle. The hammer. Dougal lifted it. His ears were on fire, and Miles's breath was hot on his face. Miles banged Dougal's head against the floor. Dougal banged the hammer against Miles's head. Their relative positions made it difficult for Dougal to get a proper swing, and it seemed to him that there was very little force behind the blow.

The hammer made contact with Miles. There was a thud, so dull as to be almost noiseless. Miles grunted. The weight on top of Dougal doubled or trebled. Miles twitched, and released one of Dougal's ears. Dougal felt as if he was being suffocated. He hit Miles a second time, this time rather more forcefully, and then once again just to make sure.

Both Dougal's ears were now free. He thought how intimately their bodies were entwined: as if they had been making love. He wriggled from underneath Miles as quickly as he could. There was a spreading dampness around the crotch of Miles's jeans. The sight of it obliterated the relief Dougal had felt.

'Please,' Dougal said. He crouched beside Miles. 'Please.'

On Miles's arm was a black digital watch. According to the display it was 20.49 on Sunday 24 May. Dougal got to his feet. He wished he could turn time back. Two minutes, or even one, would be enough. Violence always took less time than you thought it had, just as it was always messier and far more confused, both physically and emotionally, than you would have expected. And you forgot how far-reaching the effects could be, and how irrevocable.

Dougal stared at the body of Miles Provender. 'Miles,' Dougal whispered. 'Come on. Get up.'

He backed away and stood by the window. Thoughts scurried through his head. Miles was miles and miles away. He stared at Miles and rehearsed a one-sided conversation with the police.

The telephone began to ring. The sound seemed unusually loud. The police already? Without thinking, Dougal went out of the room. Staggering, as though drunk or half asleep, he crossed the hall and pushed open the kitchen door. His shoulder collided with the jamb of the doorway. He frowned. There was a telephone in a wall holster by the dresser. Dougal reached out his hand.

As his fingers touched the handset the ringing stopped. In the silence a form of sanity returned. The answering machine upstairs had cut in. He knew that he mustn't touch the phone until he had decided what to do. Killing is easy. Any fool can do it and often does. The real difficulty is what you do next.

The kitchen was full of Eleanor's paintings and drawings. They had overflowed from the notice-board to the surrounding walls, the sides of cupboards and the door of the fridge. Most of them depicted angular humanoids with huge, round eyes. All the eyes were staring at Dougal. He looked up and saw the sensor for the alarm system, which was mounted on the wall high in the corner nearest the door to the hall. The sensor had three lights, red, orange and green. They winked furiously at him – responding to the twitching of his limbs and the fluctuations of his body heat, and sending contradictory messages to his brain: STOP. GO. STOP. GO, FOR GOD'S SAKE, GO.

He opened the kitchen door and went outside. He sat down on the bench beside the path. The evening was sultry, and the smell of honeysuckle was so strong it made him feel uncomfortable. The bush sprawled across the fence that linked the corner of the house to the blank wall of the house next door. The fence separated the back garden from the drive and the front of the house.

No one could see him. See no evil. The easiest thing to do with bodies is to pretend they don't exist. What would the body be like, Dougal wondered, after three days in this heat?

It was getting harder to breathe, as though the hot, heavy air had been used so often that it was almost drained of oxygen. The honeysuckle's scent seemed to be growing stronger. The sweetness was suffocating him. He got up and leaned against the wall of the house. On the other side of the wall was the room where Miles lay. In Dougal's head the blood thumped like a drum. The brick was still warm from the sun and it was as rough as sandpaper against his cheek.

One thing was clear: he must do something. He took a deep breath and stood up, evenly balanced on his feet. An image slipped through his mind of himself bending to let a dog off its lead.

The neighbours were away. He had parked the van at the

top of the drive, which was out of sight of the road. He had told no one he was coming here this evening. Indeed he hadn't known himself until a few hours earlier. He had assumed he would have finished moving out by last night, so he hadn't objected when the duty officer had allocated him an unexpected Marital Surveillance in Northampton for Sunday afternoon and evening. But the job had folded when the protagonists were messily reconciled. There had been just enough time to drive back to London and finish the move. Dougal envied the client her reconciliation.

Must try not to be selfish. Celia said he was selfish, and he supposed it was true.

The hammer. He went into the house, back to the room that had once been his. Miles hadn't moved; that would have been too much to hope for. The corpse looked unnatural, which was absurd: a dead body was just as natural as a live one. Dougal felt hollow inside and he knew that if he went on looking at Miles he might lose whatever control he retained over the situation. He half closed his eyes and bent to pick up the hammer. The thing on the floor was no more than a blur.

Dougal left the room, crossed the hall and went into the kitchen. He lit one of the gas rings and found a big oval pan in the saucepan cupboard. He thought it was part of a contraption for poaching fish. He filled the pan with water and put it on the ring. As an afterthought he added a little household bleach.

The hammer was almost new – its rubber handle unmarked, its steel nearly stainless. Dougal couldn't face wiping it so he dropped it gently in. A pink streak rose from the head and writhed like a serpent through the water. Dougal turned away.

Doing something made him feel a little better, though he knew that boiling the hammer might not be the best way of spending his time. He opened the back door and went outside again. As he did so he realized that he had come to a decision without his noticing it. The hammer in the pan made that clear.

Much depended on whether a neighbour had seen Miles

approaching the house, or whether Miles had told anyone he was coming here. A car went down the road broadcasting country music through its open windows. Dougal shivered. Every passing car, everyone taking a dog for an evening walk, every neighbour at the window: the world was full of witnesses, all potentially hostile. He retreated into the kitchen.

By now, tiny bubbles were ascending through the water. The pink serpent had vanished.

Dougal drifted into the hall and stood listening. The heavy evening sunlight slanted through the fanlight over the front door. The house was peopled with shadows. He sensed movements just beyond his range of vision. Once or twice he thought he heard stealthy noises above his head. The atmosphere had changed since Miles's death; it even smelled different. Dougal made himself walk through the empty rooms on all three floors partly because he was frightened of the emptiness and partly to make sure the rooms were really empty.

How heavy? The question presented itself as he stood in the doorway of Eleanor's bedroom. A hundred and fifty pounds? A hundred and sixty? On the wall was an alphabet frieze: D for Dougal and Danger; H for Hash and Hammer; M for Miles and Murder. There was no way of making the weight less formidable: he would have to deal with it as a whole, not piecemeal. You needed expertise to dismember bodies. In any case Dougal lacked the courage.

In Celia's bedroom he went to the window and looked down into the front garden and the street. Nothing moved. *Mustn't forget the hash.* On the surface, his mind was calm, and thoughts moved singly and lazily: van; carpet; Cleopatra; keys; day off tomorrow; is Eleanor asleep by now?

He climbed the last flight of stairs to the attic, which Celia used as an office when she worked at home. The room had a tent-like ceiling and a row of shiny plastic machines on the desk. The warm air smelled faintly of her perfume. Tears pricked his eyes; he attributed them to self-pity, a bottomless well of emotion.

Dougal opened the bottom drawer of the filing cabinet. It contained miscellaneous stationery. He picked out a roll of parcel tape.

When he got back to the kitchen, the water was boiling. He turned down the gas to simmer and found a new pair of rubber gloves in the drawer beneath the draining board. He put them on and went outside to the garden shed. Memory had not misled him: underneath a pile of yellowing newspapers was an enormous sheet of polythene last used during Dougal's move into the Kew house when Eleanor had been just a baby. He took the polythene into the room that had once been his, taking especial care not to tread on Miles.

Not Miles now, Dougal reminded himself. Dead meat. A dead weight. Miles was miles away. He picked up the hash and Miles's set of keys. Miles and miles away.

'Concentrate,' he said aloud.

In the next hour he found it increasingly hard to believe that this mass of flesh did not still provide an earthly residence for Miles's personality in a vestigial posthumous form: the body resisted with passive malignity all Dougal's attempts to do something constructive with it. He laid out the polythene and after many failures succeeded in rolling Miles on to it with the help of a spade as a lever and a two-volume dictionary as a fulcrum. The body left a damp patch on the floorboards.

He nerved himself to search the front and back pockets of Miles's jeans. It felt a dreadfully intimate procedure, partly because the jeans were tight. The haul was meagre: a pair of keys on a ring, a scrap of yellow paper with a number scribbled on it, and a handful of change. He put these items with the hash and the other keys on the mantelpiece.

Fixing the shroud in place with parcel tape should have been easy; Dougal had almost looked forward to it. But the polythene kept slipping out of position, and the parcel tape had a tendency to split lengthways. The gloves were such a hindrance at this stage that Dougal was forced to take them off. There was no room for half-measures. He needed to pass the tape right round the body not once but three times – neck, thighs and ankles.

The neck and the ankles were relatively easy. When he came to the thighs, Dougal could have done with another pair of hands. He was forced to resort to the spade and the dictionary again and roll the body to and fro.

As he worked the light faded and his sense of urgency grew. He pushed and prodded and even kicked the body. It was curious how rapidly his fear and distaste diminished. He talked to the corpse – 'Come on, you fat toad, over you go' – cajoling, explaining and cursing. They were partners in desperation. Miles, of course, was less than human; and after a while Dougal began to feel that he was less than human too.

By the time Miles was secured, the sky was the colour of blue-black ink. Dougal drew the curtains and took the risk of turning on the light. Next, he experimented with ways of moving the body outside. This proved far harder than he had expected. In the end he was forced to redesign the lower part of the shroud. First he cut the tape round the ankles and slit the polythene up to the knees. Then he re-covered each leg separately and retaped the ankles. He reinforced this bond with a leather belt.

These modifications allowed him to hook one arm round the ankle strap and pull, while simultaneously lifting Miles's legs. He hoped that the rest of the body, that is from the haunches to the head, would simply slide across the floor. Even with his legs off the ground, however, Miles was still a considerable weight to pull, particularly when his weight met resistance, such as the pile of the fitted carpet in the hall. At this point Dougal transferred some of Miles's weight to a little wagon which belonged to Eleanor. The wagon disintegrated with a sharp cracking of plastic. In the end, brute force was the only answer – that and patience and occasional recourse to the spade and dictionary.

They moved with painful slowness through the hall and into the kitchen. As they neared the back door, Dougal glanced back and swore. Miles's head had worked itself free from the polythene and left vivid red streaks on the vinyl floor covering. Brown eyes looked at nothing and the mouth was crowded with teeth. Dougal dropped the legs and, his hands trembling with fatigue and fear, covered the head with a carrier bag from a Marks & Spencer's food hall. PLEASE RE-USE THIS BAG IN THE INTEREST OF THE ENVIRONMENT. He attached the bag to the shroud with the last of the parcel tape.

The incident unsettled him still further, and perhaps affected his co-ordination. Outside the kitchen door were two steps down to the concrete path running along the back of the house. Dougal, who was moving backwards, took them too fast; he stumbled, dropped the legs and fell on to the path. The fall jarred his spine. When he got up he found Miles slumped across the threshold. The polythene had parted under the strain, and a hairy arm had flopped on to the doormat.

'Shit,' Dougal said; and for the next few seconds he fought a powerful desire to weep at the sheer bloody-mindedness of life. But he knew that he couldn't give in now: he was much too frightened of the consequences. He was trapped in a train of events. The train hurtled along towards an unknown terminus, and there wasn't a communication cord.

He clambered over the body, found the kitchen Sellotape and patched up the shroud yet again. As if to reward him for his persistence, life treated him more kindly during the next stage of the process. Arms aching, he hauled Miles along the path. The path ran past the kitchen window and the bench to the corner of the house. It continued along the line of the six-foot-high fence until it reached the gate leading into the drive.

First Dougal, then the body crunched through a caravan of snails which had been slithering across the concrete from the lawn towards more exotic pleasures in the herb-bed at the foot of the fence. At the far end of the herb-bed was the honeysuckle bush, and beyond that was the gate.

At the end of the path, Dougal lowered Miles's legs to the

ground. He went back into his room and fetched the largest of his kilims, which he planned to use as an outer shroud. Like Cleopatra, Miles would be concealed in a carpet, though not for the same purpose.

He unbolted the gate and peered outside. The van was directly in front of him. He had planned to move his belongings out by the back door because the route was shorter and easier than by the front. For this reason he had backed the van, an unmarked Transit loaned to him by his employer, as near to the gate as he could.

The sky was now an electric blend of dark blue and orange, and the air was soft. It was a velvet London dusk at the end of a warm day. The stench of the honeysuckle was stifling. Dougal heard cars in the distance but the road itself was quiet. A television chattered somewhere on his right. The front garden and the end of the drive were beyond the effective range of the nearest streetlamp.

There was no point in waiting. Dougal hauled the body into the drive. Behind him, the gate swung shut. He unlocked the back doors of the Transit. The van was empty, because he had already unloaded the possessions removed last night. He spread the kilim on the floor. As he did so, he suddenly realized what the next problem would be: how on earth could he raise Miles a couple of feet off the ground?

Concentrate. He tried doing it by stages – first lifting the feet and shins into the van and then lifting the rest of the body. But he only succeeded in getting Miles an inch or two off the ground before the feet flopped out and Dougal's muscles gave up the struggle. He thought he might have been able to manage it if he had not been so tired. After the third attempt, the polythene gave way again. Miles's other arm slid lazily out of the shroud. Dougal decided to rest for a moment.

Simultaneously he heard footsteps coming slowly up the road. He pulled the doors together. He didn't want to shut them because he couldn't do so without making a noise. There wasn't much he could do about the body, or even himself. But this part of the drive was not visible from the road, and the Transit van should shelter them from casual glances if anyone came up to the front door. And of course the odds against this person being a visitor were enormous. His calmness surprised and pleased him.

To his horror, the footsteps slowed, as far as he could judge, at or near the mouth of the drive and stopped. Dougal cowered. Not Celia – she would have had the car and driven into the drive. Please God, he prayed, just someone lighting a cigarette or waiting for a dog to relieve itself.

God was not pleased. The footsteps continued. Now they made a different sound, for they were advancing up the gravel of the drive.

Dougal peered under the van. He glimpsed a shadowy pair of legs. Suddenly they vanished. Dougal guessed that the visitor had turned into the porch. There was a pause and then, from deep in the house, the sound of the front-door bell.

They'll realize no one is in, Dougal thought. Then they'll go away.

The bell rang a second time. After another pause, the legs emerged from the porch and stood for a few seconds. Then they advanced towards the Transit. And a light sprang out in front of them, slid under the van and glinted on the folds of polythene. The visitor had come equipped with a torch.

Fight or flight? As for a weapon, the spade was propped up by the back door. Or Dougal could escape through the house. He fumbled for the latch on the gate. He couldn't find it. Then it was too late. The beam found his legs and ran up his body. Automatically he turned towards it. The light hit his face like a blow. Behind it was a large silhouette.

'William,' James Hanbury said softly.

'What are you doing here?'

'Are you all right?'

'Yes, fine,' Dougal said. He came forward, towards the torch, towards his employer. 'Just moving my things.'

'Indeed.'

'Can I get you something?' Dougal said. 'A drink? Let's go through the front door, shall we?'

'Ah.' Hanbury took a few steps not towards the front door but towards Dougal and the fence. 'Honeysuckle, isn't it?' The torch beam swept up the fence and picked out the mass of green leaves sprinkled with long yellow, white and pink flowers. 'What a super smell.'

'Let's go inside,' Dougal said.

'I thought you were going to move yesterday,' Hanbury went on, and the beam slid from the honeysuckle to the ground. 'So I tried your new address, but you weren't there. I've got a house-warming present for you.'

'That's very kind.'

'It's a plant, a sort of cactus. They say it gets frilly pink flowers in the winter.'

Now the ungainly polythene bundle lay in a pool of light. Hanbury looked at Miles's bare, brown arm, and Dougal heard him swallow.

'Moving's a funny business, isn't it?' Hanbury said. 'Dreadfully unsettling.'

2

'A pretty pickle,' James Hanbury said.

He was standing just inside the room that had once been Dougal's. He looked relaxed, imposing and faintly nautical; he was wearing a dark blue shirt and cream trousers. The shirt was loose so that one noticed his height and the breadth of his shoulders but not the gently expanding waistline.

He pursed his lips and turned to Dougal. 'Who is it, anyway?'

Hanbury had said hardly a word since he had seen the arm. But he had helped Dougal lift the body into the van. He had watched Dougal locking the doors and had padded after him into the house.

'His name's Miles,' Dougal said, looking at the damp patch on the floor. 'He used to work for—'

'Miles Provender? Oh William, I do hope not.'

'You know him?'

'Of course I do. He's doing most of the donkey-work for the Custodemus account. Damn it, I was going to have lunch with him on Wednesday.'

'I'm sorry.'

'And it was all working out so well.'

'What was?'

'It was a trial period for everyone. I thought you knew.'

'I didn't.'

Dougal had the not unfamiliar sensation that he was living in a world where as a matter of course everyone knew more than he did. The sensation was not agreeable, but at least it made a change from having to think about damp marks on the floor or the thing in the polythene shroud: so perhaps Hanbury was merely trying to be helpful.

'Who's on trial?' Dougal asked. As he said the word 'trial', he heard himself pleading guilty to a charge of manslaughter or possibly murder.

'More or less everyone. We're giving Brassard Prentisse Communications six months to see what they can do for us. Celia's delegated most of the work to Miles. We've only just started. Hasn't she mentioned it?'

'No.'

In the last few months Dougal and Celia hadn't talked about very much except the daily decisions that sprang from sharing a house and a child; the only other subject of any importance had been the desirability of Dougal's departure. In six years Celia and Hugo Brassard had built up BPC to one of the top fifty PR companies in the UK; it was a solid achievement but there had been a price to pay. Celia's private life had shrunk. It seemed to Dougal that she still managed to find a little time for their daughter Eleanor, some but not enough; there was none left over for him.

'How very odd,' Hanbury said.

How very odd, Dougal thought: only a few yards away there was a corpse wrapped in a kilim, and here they were talking about the PR industry.

'Anyway, Miles is on trial too,' Hanbury went on. 'If he pulls his weight, I understand that Celia and Hugo are going to bump him up to associate partner. Were going, I mean. You'd better tell me what happened.'

'He got bumped off rather than up,' Dougal said, wondering what else Celia hadn't told him.

'How? Who by?'

For an instant Dougal hesitated. Attempting to mislead Hanbury could only be counter-productive: frankness might conceivably help. 'I hit him with a hammer,' he said. 'All right?'

'More like all wrong. Any particular reason?'

'I was underneath him at the time.'

'Yes, but why?'

'He was trying to pull off my ears.'

'You know what I mean. Why were you fighting?'

'It's nothing to do with you.'

Their eyes met. Dougal thought he had angered Hanbury, but he wasn't sure. Hanbury's true feelings were elusive things, as shy as unicorns. Then Hanbury grunted, perhaps because he had solved to his own satisfaction the problem of why the fight had taken place.

'What was he doing here? Can you tell me that?'

'Apparently Celia asked him to come round and do some jobs around the house.' Dougal paused to savour the bitterness. 'I was meant to move out yesterday. They thought the house would be empty.'

'So Celia's not here? That's something.'

'She's taken Eleanor up to Plumford for a few nights with Stepmum.'

They had thought the visit would make his moving out easier for Eleanor to cope with. None of this would have happened if Celia had been here.

Hanbury crossed his arms. 'So what do you propose to do?'

'If I called the police it'd be manslaughter. If I'm lucky.' Dougal hesitated, but Hanbury did not comment. 'And if I just left him here I'd be an obvious suspect. And can you imagine it? How he'd be after three days in this heat? Celia and Eleanor walking in and finding him?'

His voice trembled. He stopped talking. The thought of Eleanor stumbling into a putrefying corpse made him want to vomit. Hanbury was staring at a stack of books on the floor. His head was on one side. Perhaps he was trying to read the titles.

'And the effects would go on and on,' Dougal said. 'They'd have to move house. I think the tabloids would go for it too. Don't you?'

To Dougal's relief, Hanbury nodded slowly, and for an instant his agreement lent Dougal's decision a spurious but welcome legitimacy; then the head stopped nodding and gave a little shake instead.

'It's not quite as simple as that,' Hanbury said. 'We're forgetting something, aren't we? How this would affect you. The criminal record. The strong probability of a significant custodial sentence. Loss of job – I'm afraid there'd be no question about that. Loss of access to Eleanor. And so on and so forth.'

'I wasn't forgetting.'

'Might as well be hung for a sheep as a lamb, eh? Well, there's something in that. But what were you going to do with him?'

'I hadn't got that far.'

'Anyone know you're here?'

'No.'

'Anyone know Miles is here?'

'Celia must have been expecting him here at some point. Perhaps even this evening. But if no one actually saw him come . . .'

'Yes,' Hanbury said. 'Quite. Where's his car?'

'I don't know. I don't even know what he drives.'

'That's easy. An aubergine-coloured Vauxhall Cavalier. It's certainly not outside the house. In any case the odds are he didn't use his car. It's not as if he had far to come. So he probably walked.'

Dougal felt depressed: here it was again – everyone else knowing more than he did. 'How do you know all this?'

'By the time you'd had lunch with Miles once or twice,' Hanbury said, 'you knew an awful lot about him. In some ways more than he did himself.' He pushed back his chair and stood up.

'Are you going?' Dougal asked, hoping he had imagined the whine in his voice.

Hanbury didn't answer. He was staring around the room as if he found it as alien as Dougal did.

'There's no reason why you should get involved,' Dougal said. 'This isn't your problem, is it? Am I right in thinking you're not going to call the police?'

'Oh no. The trouble with calling the police is that you never know quite what they'll do.'

'Thank you for that.'

'I think the best thing is get rid of the body. Then Miles can just be a missing person.'

Dougal thought. 'How?'

'Give me a moment,' Hanbury said with a touch of irritation. 'I'm not a magician. First things first. Have you checked the pockets?'

'Yes. The stuff's on the mantelpiece.'

Hanbury crossed the room and examined Miles's belongings. 'Good. No car key. So he probably walked. Is that cannabis?'

'Could be,' Dougal said.

Hanbury clicked his tongue against the roof of his mouth. 'Who would have thought it? He always seemed such a clean-living sort of chap. All that rugger and so on. Still, we all have our little quirks, eh?'

'I suppose so.'

'We need a plan of action. You have to be meticulous about these things. Attention to detail, that's the key.'

'You mean you'll help me?' Dougal didn't try to disguise the relief he felt. 'Are you sure?'

'If I leave you to do it, it'll end in disaster. You're dropping with exhaustion.'

'Thank you.'

'Not at all.' Hanbury smiled brilliantly at Dougal. 'That's what friends are for. A helping hand here, a helping hand there. After all, you'd do the same for me, wouldn't you?'

There was a roaring in Dougal's ears as if a torrent were foaming through a cerebral gorge. It seemed to him that Hanbury had not meant this final question to be rhetorical: he was waiting for an answer.

'Oh yes,' Dougal heard himself say. 'Of course I would.'

Dougal thought that 'friend' was one of those words that resist definition. There were as many definitions as there were friends.

Hanbury was a friend. He was also a director of Custodemus, the security and private investigation company which employed Dougal on a part-time basis. The friendship was both encouraged and handicapped by the fact that each of them knew more about the other than the other would have liked. Dougal was one of the few people who knew that Hanbury's present success as a gamekeeper owed much to his previous experience as a poacher.

They talked little while they loaded the rest of Dougal's belongings into the van. There was too much to think about. And the more Dougal thought, the more worried he got.

When they had loaded the van, Hanbury found a small freezer bag in the kitchen. He transferred Miles's belongings, including the hash, from the mantelpiece to the bag, which he put in his pocket. He strolled in the garden and smoked a cigarette while Dougal hoovered and dusted.

When Hanbury returned, Dougal was in the empty room wiping the surfaces Miles might have touched with a dishcloth. The damp patch had vanished from the floor. The room was now a space devoid of personality.

'Everything all right?' Hanbury sounded unnaturally cheerful.

Dougal nodded. 'What now?'

'We'll keep it simple, I think. Always a temptation to be too clever. And don't worry – even if someone *has* noticed you, there's no reason why you shouldn't be here. That's the beauty of it. And there's nothing suspicious about your cleaning everything.'

'What about you?' Dougal said abruptly. 'Why did you come here? You never really explained.'

'Eh? Didn't I tell you? When I phoned in tonight, they told me the Northampton job had folded. You weren't at your new place, so I thought you'd probably be here.'

'You asked the duty officer about me?'

'No,' Hanbury said with exaggerated patience. 'He happened to mention it along with everything else. As a matter of policy, I insist on a full update twice daily.'

'Yes but—'

'It's the only way to keep tabs on things,' Hanbury continued. 'Delegate by all means, but in my opinion the manager who doesn't keep his finger on the pulse is asking for trouble.'

'Yes but what did you want me to do?'

'I don't follow.'

'There's always a reason, isn't there?'

'In this case an altruistic one.' Hanbury looked hurt, and possibly was. 'I knew you were moving, knew something of the circumstances – I thought perhaps this might be the moment when you'd appreciate a friendly face.' Hanbury glanced round the room. His nostrils briefly flared. He achieved the difficult feat of raising one eyebrow but not the other. 'And it looks as if I was right, doesn't it?'

'I'm sorry.'

'It doesn't matter. You're overtired, which isn't surprising.'

Dougal nodded. At present he felt as though he would stay awake for ever. Nor did he want to sleep. He was afraid of dreaming.

'We're making excellent progress. We've almost completed phase one. Is there anything else you need do before we leave?'

'Just set the burglar alarm and lock up.'

The controls for the burglar alarm were in the hall. Hanbury watched as Dougal reset the system. It was a relatively unsophisticated model, now discontinued, which Dougal had bought at a substantial discount through Custodemus, whose home security division marketed it for the manufacturers. Operating it would have confused a stranger, Dougal thought, because you had an apparent choice between using the electronic number pad or a key. A stranger wouldn't have known that the number pad was so temperamental that the engineer had mounted an old-fashioned manual lock in parallel. A stranger wouldn't have known that they never used the number pad. But of course Miles wasn't a stranger.

Dougal imagined Miles and Celia standing shoulder to shoulder while Celia explained. Jealousy twisted inside him.

Celia wouldn't show a mere colleague how to disable her burglar alarm. She wouldn't give a stranger the keys to her house. Keys and burglar alarms were very intimate things. They controlled access to a home and hence to a person's privacy. For the first time Dougal realized how close Miles must have got to Celia. What made it worse was the fact that Celia hadn't had the courage to be frank about it. Dougal hated the thought that she had not wanted to hurt his feelings. It would have been easier to bear if she had said, 'I want you out of the house because I've found someone else.' It was too late for her to do so now. Miles was miles away. Miles and miles and miles—

'William.' Hanbury touched Dougal's shoulder. 'Come along.'

It was after eleven by the time they left the house. The road was quiet. Hanbury said that he had left the Jaguar a couple of streets away: he had not liked to park in the drive in case Celia was at home and did not want to be disturbed, and her road was residents-only parking. Hanbury walked round the van.

'It's filthy,' he said approvingly. 'Very difficult to read the number plates. Have you got the keys? If you don't mind, I think I'll drive.'

Dougal climbed into the passenger seat. He stared at the windscreen until Hanbury reminded him to put on his seat belt.

Hanbury started the engine and drove slowly on to the road. The houses opposite Celia's and on either side were in darkness. Sensible people lived in all of them. The road as a whole was bursting at the seams with sensible people. They were getting a good night's sleep before the rigours of the working week.

They drove up to Kew Bridge. There was relatively little traffic at this time of night on a Sunday evening, and it was a short and familiar drive over the river and on to the M4. Once they reached the motorway, the van rattled along in the slow lane. Dougal rolled down his window and the night air chilled his skin. Even with Miles and the residue of Dougal's

23

possessions, the back of the van was less than half full. The air rushed through the emptiness and made a dull booming sound like distant breakers on a stormy night.

Dougal sat well forward in his seat. Occasionally he glanced to his right: in profile Hanbury's face was stern and distinguished. Dougal's head ached. His eyes were dry and felt larger than usual. Part of his mind seemed to have fallen asleep: he knew he was awake but the waking world had become the backdrop to an unpleasant dream. He was scared to look over his shoulder in case Miles had unwrapped himself and was advancing wrathfully from the back of the van.

A steady trickle of cars overtook them. Dougal watched the taillights dwindling. Red for danger, he thought. He had lost all sense of time. He was too tired to look at his watch, too tired to lean forward to read the clock on the dashboard.

'Where we going?' he said.

'Not far,' Hanbury said. 'We'll take the next turn-off.'

Dougal tried closing his eyes. It didn't help. A change in the engine note alerted him. He saw a signpost that said 'Slough'. Soon Hanbury was driving through a built-up area. It was obvious that he knew exactly where he was going. Dougal closed his eyes again and saw Miles's smiling face.

'Piss off,' Dougal muttered.

'What was that?' Hanbury said.

'Nothing.'

With an effort of will Dougal wiped Miles away. All was darkness in front of his eyes. He wished it were a bottomless pit into which he could throw himself. He imagined himself eternally falling. Perhaps the motion would be soothing. Perhaps if you were falling endlessly, you would adapt to your new environment and eventually be able to sleep.

'Nearly there,' a voice said cheerfully.

Dougal opened his eyes. They were driving through what looked like an industrial estate past its prime. The place was deserted. Many of the buildings were decorated with 'To Let' signs. Suddenly a chain-mesh fence appeared. The fence was topped with a triple line of barbed wire. Hanbury turned left into a narrower road, and the fence turned left with them. Dougal noticed that the fence was in very poor condition.

Hanbury glanced at Dougal. 'It's an enormous site,' he said, speaking slowly as if the information was tremendously important. 'They pulled down most of the old factory and then they couldn't afford to build a new one.'

Dougal shut his eyes again. Miles smirked at him. Honk, honk. Miles was miles away, so Dougal was miles away too, so Miles was Dougal: true or false? The van slowed. Dougal swayed to his right which meant the van was turning left. He half opened his eyes and glimpsed or dreamed a weatherbeaten but familiar sign. On it was the legend:

CUSTODEMUS

24 hours a day, 7 days a week, 365 days a year.

Permanent peace of mind.

'Peace has a price,' Hanbury said, whether in real life or in Dougal's dream. 'Unfortunately the owners stopped paying it. We've had to take them to court.'

They drove on without lights. The van bumped in and out of potholes. Sometimes the tyres slithered over gravel. The van jerked and the engine roared as Hanbury felt his way about the strange gearbox. Dougal squeezed his eyelids together so not a particle of light could slip between them. But Miles's face was equipped with its own source of illumination.

Suddenly the van was no longer moving. The engine coughed and died.

'Well,' Hanbury said. 'Here we are.'

Dougal opened his eyes. For a moment he could not interpret what he saw. Dreams were often like that. The van's sidelights were now on. The van was not outside any more because there was no longer a reflected yellow glow from the sky. They were in a large building with bare brick walls. Quite old, Dougal thought, and apparently windowless. The roof was invisible.

Directly in front of them was an elderly Ford Escort. It had four doors and a roof rack. The light was too poor for Dougal to be able to identify its colour.

'It's stolen, of course,' Hanbury said. He climbed down from the van and opened one of the back doors of the Escort. He looked up at Dougal. 'Come along. I'll need your help.'

Dougal joined Hanbury at the back of the van. Hanbury opened the doors and pulled back the kilim. And there was Miles. Or rather there was the polythene-shrouded, sausage-shaped bundle with the Marks & Spencer carrier bag covering the nearer end. SAFETY FIRST. TO AVOID DANGER OF SUFFOCATION KEEP THIS WRAPPER AWAY FROM BABIES AND CHILDREN.

'You take the legs, eh?'

Hanbury clasped the bundle just below the shoulders. He pulled. Hanbury was surprisingly strong. The body moved out of the van. Hanbury must have been supporting all the weight above the knees. Miles's knees.

'William! I said take the legs.'

Dougal slipped his arm into the loop made by the belt binding the ankles.

'Good man. Off we go.'

They staggered across the few yards of concrete that separated the van from the Escort. Hanbury rested the top half of the body on the seat. Dougal, still holding the legs, waited while Hanbury went round the other side of the car and opened the door. Then Hanbury pulled and Dougal pushed.

'He's too long,' Hanbury said. 'You'll have to bend the legs. No, more than that. A bit to the right. Super. See if you can shut your door.'

Dougal had to lean against the door to make it close because the feet were trying to escape. Hanbury slammed the door on his side and led the way back to the van. Dougal wondered what was going to happen next, but he didn't like to ask.

Hanbury started the engine and reversed the van into the open air. There was a yellow glow on the horizon, but between the van and the horizon was a broad cordon of darkness. Hanbury cut the engine and the lights.

'Wait here,' he said. 'I won't be long.'

Dougal waited. He sat shivering somewhere between waking and sleeping. Overhead he saw the navigation lights of a plane moving sluggishly across the sky; but there was a curious absence of sound. It was as if life were going on all around him, but he was no longer attached to it; as if he were enclosed in a glass bubble. After several minutes, perhaps longer, the driver's door opened and Hanbury climbed in. A smell of petrol filled the van. Hanbury started the engine, rammed it into gear and drove into the cordon of darkness.

Dougal shut his eyes again. Miles was there. But Miles was miles away. So Dougal was miles away. So Dougal must be Miles.

3

When the doorbell rang Dougal naturally assumed it was the police.

At the time he was standing in front of the long mirror on the wardrobe door. It was a little after seven o'clock on Monday evening. He had just made the unwelcome discovery that the waistband of his only suit had mysteriously shrunk. He sucked in his stomach and did up the buttons. Underneath the white shirt the sweat pricked his skin. He licked his lips.

'Yes, my name's William Dougal . . . Miles who?'

No – pretending that he didn't know Miles Provender could be foolish. They had met three or four times in the last few months, usually before witnesses, beginning with the disastrous Brassard Prentisse Christmas party at the end of last year. It had been dislike at first sight but no need to mention that.

The doorbell rang again. They were getting impatient.

The big, high room was full of evening light. It poured through the tall north window and down from the row of grimy skylights. An oven in summer, a refrigerator in winter. At least he wouldn't be here in winter. Jails would have central heating.

The middle of the room was occupied by a hillock of cardboard boxes and black plastic sacks. Dougal picked his way between it and the double bed, which was no longer made up. He stumbled twice and wondered if he had ever felt so weary. His coordination was appalling today. But he managed to keep well away from the bed. As he moved he scratched his ribs.

The mattress was like a plateau crowded with interesting topographical features. A deep crevice ran down its centre. There were literally dozens of dips, lumps and stains. The only thing on top of the mattress was a small, dusty Christmas cactus in an orange plastic pot.

Dougal had slept for only a few hours on Saturday night. The itching had started then. He had put it down to the heat and perhaps a few mosquito bites. Last night, after disposing of Miles, the itching had been of an entirely different order. At first Dougal had almost welcomed it as a distraction from his memories. Soon, however, it built itself up to an intolerable level and became not a distraction from undesirable memories but a sort of physical counterpoint to them. Dougal had got out of bed, switched on the light and made the discovery that the plateau was populated with small, reddish-brown monsters which had gorged themselves on his blood.

A curtained doorway led to a small kitchen like a ship's galley. The room smelled because the previous tenant had left behind not only the bedbugs but a half-used carton of milk. At the end of the kitchen were two doors. One led, in defiance of planning regulations, directly to a combined lavatory and shower room. Dougal opened the other door and prepared to go quietly.

There, standing on the wooden platform at the top of the short flight of steps, was Celia Prentisse.

'What are you doing here?' Dougal said.

Almost imperceptibly she recoiled as though he had offered to hit her.

'I'm sorry,' Dougal said. 'I wasn't expecting you. Come in.'

She followed him through the kitchen and into the studio. She was wearing a dark skirt and a white top – office clothes – and carrying a shoulder bag. He looked back and saw her wrinkling her nose.

'A bit of a tip, I'm afraid.' Suddenly he was tired of being apologetic; also, he was desperate to avoid questions about his moving out of the Kew house. 'I thought you weren't coming back to London till Thursday.'

'Hugo phoned this morning. A major crisis.'

There was a hint of a smile on her face. Hugo Brassard was

her partner. He always seemed to have a crisis when Celia was away, and the crises were always major, at least in his estimation. But Dougal refused the invitation to share an old joke. He thought it was more likely that Celia had come back early because she was pining for Miles.

'Couldn't Hugo cope?' he asked.

'Not really. This time it really was urgent.'

'Where's Eleanor?'

'I left her at Plumford. Margaret was over the moon.'

Margaret was Celia's stepmother, and life had no greater pleasure for her than undisturbed possession of Eleanor.

'Is that wise?' Dougal said, and instantly wished he could cancel the question.

'What's wrong with it?'

'I thought the idea was—'

'Ideas change,' Celia said. 'Eleanor and Margaret will have a lovely time together. Besides I haven't any choice. I told you: it was urgent.'

'You could have asked me.'

'She couldn't stay here, could she?' Celia looked around the room. 'I'm surprised you can.'

'It'll be different when I've sorted things out.'

'And it's not as if we've got a reliable child-minder. Besides, it won't do Eleanor any harm to be spoiled for a few days. It is her half-term, after all.'

Dougal glanced at his watch. He was going to be late. Hanbury had made a point of asking him to be punctual. Celia wasn't looking at him. She sat down in the armchair where Dougal had spent most of last night.

'To be honest,' she went on, 'I was glad to get away. You know what Margaret's like.'

'Easier to appreciate at a safe distance?'

Their eyes met. Dougal wondered whether she put him in that category too.

'Exactly. By the way, Eleanor sent you a drawing.'

Celia opened the shoulder bag and took out a sheet of paper, which she gave to Dougal. On it was a felt-tip picture of a house with a door, four squarish windows and a rather dashing purple roof. At the top was written 'daddy's new house'. To one side of the main picture were three figures in a line, a man and a woman with a little girl holding their hands.

'Amazingly sophisticated,' Dougal said. 'She's put in knee joints and elbows and shoelaces with bows. And did you notice, the man's got stubble?'

For a moment they were united in admiration of Eleanor. Dougal thought the picture was sophisticated in another sense, and no doubt Celia did as well: as an attempt to make life imitate art.

'She wanted you to have it right away,' Celia said. 'That's one reason I came round.'

Dougal looked up. 'And the other?'

Perhaps a neighbour had seen something last night.

Celia dug into the bag once more. 'Look what I found in the kitchen.' She took out Dougal's wallet. He stared stupidly at it. 'Haven't you missed it since Saturday?'

'No.' Dougal took it: driving licence, credit cards, cash. Without money he couldn't have got to the West End this evening. If he had left his wallet behind last night, what other mistakes might he have made? He felt surrounded by invisible traps of his own making. He heard himself speaking: 'I haven't been shopping yet. Only to get a paper.'

The *Evening Standard* was on the table beside the chair. Dougal had read it from cover to cover. He was absolutely sure that it didn't contain a report of a mysterious fatality in the vicinity of Slough. Maybe the body hadn't been found. Maybe he had dreamed the whole thing.

'Anyway, thanks for bringing it.' He added in the hope that it would explain why he hadn't missed the wallet: 'There's been a lot to sort out here.'

'So I see. You've got the week off work?'

'Just today and tomorrow.'

Neither of them spoke for a moment and that was worse

than talking because during silences you invent your own conversations.

'Can I get you something?' Dougal asked. It felt unnatural to be offering hospitality to Celia. How many years had they shared a house, on and off? Four? Five? 'Some tea? A drink?'

'No, thanks.'

After another silence they both began to talk at once. They stopped simultaneously in mid-sentence.

'You first,' Celia said.

'No – after you.'

'I'm not keeping you, am I? You look as if you're going out.'

'There's no hurry. Actually I was wondering where I put my ties.'

Dougal bent down and undid one of the black plastic sacks. If only he had had the sense to label them. This sack seemed to contain nothing but odd socks.

'Didn't Margaret give you a tie at Christmas?' Celia said. 'Blue with white spots. Italian silk.'

'Yes. But I'm not sure where it is.'

He noticed that Celia hadn't asked him where he was going. It was none of her business. He wasn't sure whether he was glad, sorry or indifferent. He knew that she didn't have much time for James Hanbury, employer and friend in need.

'There's something hanging out of the side pocket of that bag,' Celia said. 'The canvas one.'

'What were you going to say?'

'I was only going to ask if you'd like some plants here. A sort of house-warming present, perhaps. I noticed the cactus.'

'I think it's dead,' Dougal said. 'Or at least terminally ill.'

He tugged at the bag. It was partly covered by a small mound of black sacks projecting like a fungoid offshoot from the main hillock. The movement dislodged not only the sacks, spilling some of their contents, but also the kilim which last night had concealed Miles.

'I'd forgotten how pretty that kilim was,' Celia said.

'Yes it is.'

'It'd look nice in the middle of the room. Add a bit of colour. And it would cover up most of that ghastly carpet.'

'Good idea.'

'Sorry. It's nothing to do with me.'

'All suggestions are welcome,' Dougal said. 'Do carry on. I'd be grateful. Really.'

He pulled out the tie from the bag. It was plain grey, suitable for weddings, and badly in need of ironing. He thought Celia was looking critically at it. He turned away and knotted it in front of the wardrobe. The tie had a small stain of what looked like tomato ketchup.

'This place needs more than a kilim, I'm afraid,' Celia went on. 'You really need to redecorate completely. But it's certainly got potential. What was it? An artist's studio?'

'I think so. Something like that. But that was years ago.'

'Is there more I haven't seen?'

'There's a sort of garden shed underneath. But I haven't got the use of that.'

For a few minutes they held a stilted conversation about Dougal's new home, which was a curious building perhaps a hundred years old and constructed largely of wood on brick foundations. It leaned against the back wall of the narrow garden of a terraced house. The outside staircase led down to a gate giving on to an alley behind the gardens of the terrace. The Goldhawk Road was five minutes' walk away.

Together with the house and garden, the studio was owned by one of Dougal's colleagues at Custodemus. The woman was having trouble with her mortgage, so she let the studio to a series of short-term tenants, the latest of whom was Dougal. It was a strictly cash-only arrangement, partly because no one seriously believed the studio was fit for human habitation.

'But at least that means it's cheap,' Dougal said. He decided not to mention the bedbugs in case it seemed like a bid for sympathy.

Celia said nothing. He picked up the jacket and put it on. He looked at himself in the mirror. A stranger looked back.

Andrew Taylor

Usually he enjoyed the rare occasions when he wore a suit. A suit made him feel as if he was playing a different part, a more respectable role than life usually allotted him. Like a uniform or a disguise, it absolved him from personal responsibility. He dabbed ineffectually at the bits of fluff on the shoulders.

'Very nice,' Celia said drily.

He saw her face in the mirror. She was smiling at him. The old smile, the old Celia, the old hope that the past could somehow be redeemed. He swung round but the smile was gone and the woman in the chair was beyond his reach again: a successful businesswoman and working mother; a woman with different standards and interests from his.

She stood up. 'I must be off. Can I give you a lift?'

'You're going' – he had almost said 'home' but he saw the pitfall at the last moment – 'to Kew?'

'Yes. But I can drop you at a station if you're going the other way.'

'No thanks,' Dougal said. 'I've got a few things to do before I leave.'

He saw her to the door. She walked down the wooden steps. At the bottom she looked up. She didn't smile or wave, but at least she looked at him. Then she went through the gate into the alley.

Celia was going back to Kew. She was going there because she hoped Miles would come to her. Was it possible, Dougal wondered, to be jealous of a ghost?

34

4

'Mr Hanbury?' the porter wheezed. 'I don't recall the name. Not offhand, that is.'

'I was meant to be meeting him here at seven forty-five,' Dougal said.

It was five past eight by the big clock above the porter's desk.

'Then it looks like your Mr Hanbury's late.'

'No message then?'

'I'm afraid not.'

'Perhaps I could wait.'

The red-rimmed eyes looked sharply at him. 'I dare say. If you'd like to take a seat.' The old man nodded towards a group of chairs.

'Is there a phone I could use first?'

'You'll find a pay phone in the booth behind you.'

Dougal went into the booth and closed the door. He was bathed in sweat. The suit was far too warm for a hot May evening, particularly if you had jogged all the way from Green Park underground station. The Royal Commonwealth Institute was in Green Place, a cul-de-sac off St James's Street. Though it was primarily a charitable organization, the RCI helped to pay its bills by encouraging its members to use its palatial London headquarters as a club. Hanbury had recently joined, and was exploring its amenities with endearing enthusiasm.

Dougal dialled the number from memory. The phone was answered at the second ring.

'Yes?' a voice whispered.

'Margaret? It's William. How are you?'

There was a sharp intake of air at the other end. 'I've only just got Eleanor settled,' Margaret hissed. 'I just hope the phone hasn't woken her. What is it?'

'I wondered if I could have a word with her.'

'Quite out of the question,' Celia's stepmother said, forgetting to whisper. 'She's exhausted. In my opinion she's allowed to stay up far too late. Children her age need at least twelve hours of sleep.'

'Could you say that I phoned? And thank her for the picture. I liked it very much.'

'What's this Celia tells me about you moving out?'

'It's just a trial—'

'If you ask me, it's time you two stopped being selfish and got married. You should think of Eleanor for a change.'

A woman hobbled through the doorway. She was small, blonde and very attractive. Her left leg was in plaster, and she was on crutches. The old porter started forward to help in some urgent if unspecified way. A younger colleague appeared from nowhere on the same errand.

'I do think of her,' Dougal said. 'Really.'

James Hanbury appeared behind the woman. He fended off the porters with a wave of the newspaper in his hand.

'You should do more than think. If you ask me, you—'

'Love to you both,' Dougal interrupted. 'I must go.'

He put down the phone and pushed open the door. Hanbury gave him a nod. He guided the woman to a chair and helped her sit down. The porters retired behind their desk and kept an eye on proceedings.

'This is William Dougal, my dear,' Hanbury said. 'Joan Trotwood.'

Hanbury left a tiny gap between Joan's Christian name and surname, as if he had paused to select the latter from a list of possible candidates. Joan smiled up at Dougal and held out her hand. She was older than she had looked from a distance – about forty, perhaps, rather than fifteen years younger – but just as attractive.

'I'll sign you in,' Hanbury said.

Joan grinned at Dougal. 'We're late, aren't we?' She had a throaty voice with flattened vowels. 'It's all my fault. Everything takes twice as long with this bloody plaster. It's like a ball and chain.'

Hanbury bustled towards them. 'I thought we'd go outside.'

The garden was at the back of the building. In the rich evening sunlight it looked so immaculate it might have been enamelled; beyond it, behind a cordon of trees, high iron railings and bushes, was Green Park itself.

The lawn was dotted with tables and chairs. Hanbury led the way to a table that stood away from the others in a corner of the garden. No sooner had the three of them settled themselves than a waitress appeared with a bottle of Bollinger in an ice bucket, followed by a second waitress with glasses and bowls of nuts, followed by a third bearing menus. Hanbury's talent for organization had been at work. Dougal wondered what it had cost.

When they were alone again, Hanbury raised his glass.

'Let us begin with a toast,' he said, glancing at Joan. 'Now what would be appropriate? Absent friends? Perhaps not. What about Austerford? May it bring us success.'

'Austerford,' he and Joan said, and drank.

'Austerford?' Dougal asked.

'You'll see,' Hanbury said.

Dougal drank. Hanbury had laid his newspaper on the table. It was an *Evening Standard*. Judging by the different headline, it was a later edition than the one Dougal had bought. Hanbury casually folded the paper so the stop-press column was on top. There was a small item which had not been in the earlier edition. It was headed 'Factory Fire'.

'Where did you find this place?' Joan asked. 'It's like something out of Noel Coward.'

'The fellow who handles our PR put me on to it. Miles Provender. Nice chap.' Hanbury glanced at Dougal, who was trying to read the newspaper. 'Have you met him, William?'

He turned back to Joan and added parenthetically. 'Miles works for Celia, who's a very old friend of William's.'

Dougal nodded and smiled. Unwillingly he admired the professionalism of Hanbury's choice of tenses. He drank and smiled again. The smile felt glazed into position. While he smiled and drank he read the stop-press column upside down. There was no mention of a burned-out car with the remains of a body on its back seat: just a blaze, and arson was suspected. He was about to have another sip when he noticed that his glass was empty. Hanbury was already reaching for the bottle.

'What a delightful way to spend a summer evening. Friends and a bottle of wine in a garden. What could be better?'

The second glass went the way of the first, and then there was a second bottle and they were ordering their dinner. A wine waiter appeared and Hanbury had a long discussion with him about the respective merits of a 1985 Beaune Marconnets and a 1984 Ruchottes Chambertin before Hanbury summed up in favour of the former ('I want a big, chewy wine tonight'). But Dougal must have misheard Hanbury's instructions to the wine waiter because during the meal, which was served outside in the gradually gathering darkness, they drank both bottles of burgundy. There was also a 1976 Beerenauslese, though afterwards Dougal remembered not so much its flavour as the words on its label, which Hanbury read out in full, the long Germanic syllables rolling through the twilight like an invocation or a curse.

'Ah,' Hanbury went on, 'the long hot summer of 1976. I remember it well.' He patted Joan's arm, which lay, plump and appetizing, on the table beside his. 'The summer we met, my love.'

There were other diners and drinkers in the garden that evening, but as the light faded away, so did Dougal's awareness of their presence. He knew he was drinking too much. He didn't want to stop. The alcohol was carrying him upwards like a lift, miles and miles away from the memories in the basement.

Joan laughed a great deal and during the second bottle of burgundy Dougal found himself laughing too. She laughed at what he said, tempting him to amuse her with more jokes. For a while Dougal felt flattered. Then he began to suspect that there was nothing personal in her laughter, that anyone could have made her laugh because she needed to laugh for some obscure reason of her own. A moment later it belatedly occurred to him that she might have set out deliberately to flatter him.

He stopped talking. He watched Hanbury stepping smoothly into the breach. Soon she was laughing again. Dougal tried the Beerenauslese and it tasted both sickly and sour; he pushed the glass away. The darker it became the more the bites of the bedbugs itched.

Later still, Joan's and Hanbury's cigarettes glowed in the darkness and scented the night air. They drank cup after cup of coffee. Hanbury and Joan ordered brandy, but Dougal declined. He noticed that Hanbury barely touched his own glass.

'Austerford,' Hanbury said, pouring Joan another cup of coffee.

'Must we talk about Georgie, darling?'

Joan lent her head against Hanbury's shoulder. The stream of coffee wavered but did not splash on to the saucer.

'Oh yes,' Hanbury said. 'William's going to help us, dear. Won't you, William?'

Dougal's tongue was thick and heavy in his mouth. 'Yes,' he croaked. *That's what friends are for.* He scratched his ribcage and wished he could rest his head on the table and try to go to sleep. Except that he wouldn't sleep.

'I knew I could rely on you,' Hanbury said. 'You won't regret it, I promise you that.' His cigarette fluttered in the darkness as he patted Joan. 'Shall I tell him? Or will you?'

'You tell him,' Joan said, her voice suddenly harsh. 'For Christ's sake, you do it.'

For a moment no one said anything. Hanbury edged his chair near Joan's and slipped his arm round her shoulders.

'Georgie,' Hanbury said. 'When Joan and I knew him he was Georgie Trotwood. But he wasn't that before, and he won't be that now. God knows what his name was originally: I'm trying to find out. But it's a fair bet that he still calls himself Georgie. He's about my age, about six foot three, thin, balding at the front, slight stoop, blue-grey eyes.'

'Big mouth,' Joan said. 'Thin lips.'

'He's got one of those accents that could come from anywhere. I knew him first. We used to see each other at the same places. Not often, maybe once a fortnight, once a month. Georgie fancied himself as a backgammon player in those days. He seemed to be very well off – property interests, he said, here and abroad. I wouldn't say we were close. Anyway, to cut a long story short, there came an evening when someone introduced him to Joan. It was after she and I'd stopped living together—'

'You'd gone and got married,' Joan said, punching his side.

'A temporary aberration,' Hanbury said. 'The upshot was, I didn't see Joan or Georgie for a while. Next thing I knew Joan sent me a Christmas card from Spain. Georgie had retired, Joan said in the card, and they were going to get married, and they were living near Marbella with their butler—'

'That was a joke,' Joan interrupted.

'Yes . . . Well I never saw the villa in the flesh. Just photographs. Very much what you'd expect but more so. Dobermanns and wrought-iron balconies and swimming pools. You know the sort of thing.'

Hanbury stopped talking. Joan's face was a blur across the table. Dougal thought he heard a sigh and a sniff. Suddenly he realized that Joan was crying.

'Oh my dear,' Hanbury said. 'I'm sorry. But William has to know anything that might be relevant.'

'It doesn't matter,' Joan said. 'The toad.'

'What do you want dee to moo?' Dougal asked, feeling it was time he made his presence felt. 'Me to do.' He frowned, sensing that he might not have made his meaning as clear as he would have liked.

'Eh?' Hanbury now had Joan on his knee. Her arms clung round his neck. 'Georgie's reneged on his agreement.'

'The bastard conned me,' said Joan, her voice muffled. 'Marriage? That's a laugh. Kept putting it off, didn't he? I did everything to try and – oh, what does it matter? The point is, he got tired of me. And now he's got someone else. He said he hadn't but he has. I could smell the bitch on his skin. Anyway, we had a fight. And he chucked me out.'

'Quite literally, I'm afraid, with a little help from Franky-Boy.' Hanbury lit another cigarette. 'I mentioned there were balconies, you remember? Hence the broken leg.'

'He said if he sees me again, he's going to get Franky-Boy to break the other one. And he would too.' Joan bounced on Hanbury's lap. 'I give him six years of my life and what does he give me? Sod all.'

'Who's Franky-Boy?' Dougal asked.

'The quasi-butler,' Hanbury said. 'More quasi than butler, I gather.'

'He's like Georgie's dog. He's not right in the head. There's something missing.'

'Darling, you're trembling. What is it?'

'Franky-Boy will do anything for Georgie. Anything. And he likes it when it's rough. Do you understand?'

'Yes,' Hanbury said. 'But don't you worry about Franky-Boy, my love.' He leaned closer to Dougal. 'It's Georgie we're concerned with. He's vanished. The villa's empty and on the market.'

'He owes me,' Joan said. 'Alimony, palimony, damages, medical and travel expenses. You name it, he owes me it.'

'Yes, my love. We don't want to be greedy, William, so we're thinking in terms of four hundred thousand pounds. I think you'll agree it's a not unreasonable price for these terrible emotional and physical scars, and for those lost years of her life.'

'But will he pay?' Dougal asked. He wondered what Hanbury's commission would be.

'We think so. He can certainly afford it. And Joan has a little lever.'

'Not so little,' Joan said. 'And all it would take is a phone call.'

'It's not quite as simple as that, dearest. We have to find him first. And also we have to make it appear that the leverage is coming from a different direction. Otherwise it may not be just a leg that gets broken.'

'He'll go mad,' Joan said happily. 'He'll be sick as a bloody parrot. He'll—'

'But he's not going to know who's applying the pressure,' Hanbury interrupted.

'For all he'll know it could be one of the victims,' Joan said. 'Or one of their children. When Osmond-Mac—'

'The point is,' Hanbury said, 'he has no idea that Joan knows about this lever. So his tantrums won't matter. They won't have a target. But we'll deal with that later. The important thing now is Georgie's location. William? William?'

'What?' Dougal dragged back his attention from the rustling leaves, the half-heard conversations of other diners and the constant undertow of anxiety.

'You seemed miles away,' Hanbury said.

'I'm listening.'

'It so happened I had lunch with Georgie a few months before this blew up. He didn't know that Joan and I were still in touch – it's something we've tended to keep under wraps. In fact he doesn't know that we were ever more than acquaintances. And from what he said I rather gathered he was planning to start some sort of business in this country. If anything, of course, that will increase our leverage.'

'Assuming you find him,' Dougal said, wanting to make a contribution while he was still able to concentrate. He tried desperately to moisten the inside of his mouth.

'You'll be pleased to hear that we have a very good idea of where he may be.'

'Wonderful,' Dougal said. 'Well, that's it. Happy ending. And very well deserved, if I may say so.'

He drained his cup and spilled a few drops of coffee on his

shirt and tie. He had hoped the coffee would sober him up, but it seemed to have had the opposite effect.

'We think he's living at a place called Austerford,' Hanbury said. 'Possibly under the name of Sutcombe. Austerford's only about fifty miles away. Do you think you could trot down there and find out what he's up to? And perhaps get a photo of him for absolute confirmation?'

'Well, yes – I—'

'Splendid.'

'You're a darling,' said Joan, and through the darkness came the sound of her blowing a moist kiss across the table.

Dougal swallowed once again. 'But—'

'I know,' Hanbury said. 'You've just moved house. Tomorrow's your day off. No problem. There's no reason why you shouldn't go down on Wednesday instead. What does another day matter?'

Dougal struggled to his feet. He held on to the table. There were lots of problems. There were problems everywhere he looked. A glass shattered somewhere around his feet. He swayed forward over the table, pushed himself backwards and almost overbalanced; but he did not fall. He was aware that most of the conversations at other tables had stopped. It was much cooler now. He shivered. He had something very important to say.

'Days always matter,' he announced.

'Are you all right?' Hanbury said.

'Could you get me a taxi? I think I'd better go home.'

'Of course, dear boy. You must be shattered.'

Another glass broke. Waitresses fluttered like magpies towards their table.

'I'm perfectly all right,' Dougal said. He let go of the table and straightened up. 'I just teed a naxi.'

5

Osmond Mac, when are you coming back? Ooh – ooh . . . Osmond Mac, when are you coming back? Ooh – ooh . . .

The tune went round and round and the words kept asking their unanswerable question. Motown music, Dougal thought, an old, old song which he'd never liked very much, and now it was making his headache worse; but not Motown because the words weren't right and the only instrument he could hear was the telephone; and who the hell was Osmond Mac?

The words went away and only the telephone was left. Buzz buzz, like an electronic bee. Buzz buzz, bugger off. Why hadn't the answering machine cut in with Celia's voice, cool and calm: 'We are sorry that no one is at present available to take your call . . .'?

The world beyond his lashes was unbearably bright. Very gradually, he widened the gaps between his eyelids. He saw what looked like a monstrous green spider with an orange belly and far more legs than were natural. It was squatting on the bare mattress of the bed. He knew he should do something about it. The buzzing continued. He knew he should do something about that too. He had forgotten that he had a telephone. He had forgotten many other things too. He could feel the crowds of unwanted memories gathering on the borders of his consciousness. He wondered how long he had been like this – suspended between waking and sleeping in a light-filled place with pains in his head and his back and that damned song circling like a vulture.

Not a spider, he thought – a Christmas cactus.

Dougal opened his eyes. The crowds rushed in. He was

wearing a navy-blue nylon sleeping bag and sitting in the armchair. His legs were resting on a pile of black plastic sacks topped by the kilim which had once covered Miles. He sat up and swung his legs off the pile. The pains multiplied and grew worse. His mouth was parched. He stood up. The sleeping bag fell to his knees. He discovered that he was naked. Where, he wondered, was the phone?

He stumbled out of the sleeping bag and staggered towards the kitchen door. As he moved he realized that part of him still knew what another part of him had forgotten: that the telephone was somewhere on the shelves over the table. The shelves were invisible because a jumble of his possessions was in the way. He pulled aside a heap of towels. A cardboard box fell to the ground with the tinkle of china.

'Oh,' Dougal said, surprised rather than annoyed.

He remembered a glass breaking last night. Or had he dreamed it? In his mind it was somehow linked with Osmond Mac (when are you coming back?). He snatched the handset of the phone. The cord was tangled so the base followed. It banged against his crotch.

'You shit,' he squealed.

'I beg your pardon,' said James Hanbury.

'Granted, I'm sure,' Dougal snarled. He sat down heavily on the bed. The cactus toppled over, depositing a heap of dried earth on the mattress. 'What time is it?'

'Nearly midday. I'm sorry to disturb you on your day off.'

Glancing idly downwards, Dougal saw the clusters of angry red bites among the black hairs of his white skin. Suddenly he realized where he was sitting. He stood up quickly. Pain lanced above his right eyebrow. Presumably one could buy powders and sprays to deal with this sort of insect infestation. He hoped such things would be on open display, that it wouldn't be necessary to ask for them. He imagined how the shop assistant would examine him with horrified curiosity and keep his or her distance to avoid contamination. Life was full of such petty humiliations.

'William? Are you still there?'

'More or less. What is it?'

'It seems there's a bit of a flap at Brassard Prentisse.'

Everything became very quiet. Dougal heard the distant roar of traffic on the Goldhawk Road. He was fully alert now, thanks to the miraculously reviving powers of adrenalin.

'I've just been talking to Celia,' Hanbury went on. 'You know Miles Provender, don't you? Apparently he's disappeared.'

Dougal said nothing because there was nothing he could usefully say. He wanted a glass of water. He leaned against the table and breathed very deeply. On top of the pile of towels was the drawing which Celia had brought him yesterday evening: Eleanor's view of her father's new home and her happy family holding hands outside it.

'Miles was meant to be setting up an interview for me yesterday,' Hanbury explained. 'The *Independent*'s doing a feature on private investigation and security firms, and it was going to focus on Custodemus. In the bag, Miles said. But I didn't hear a word from him. So I phoned Brassard Prentisse this morning and found the whole place in turmoil.'

'Just . . . just because of Miles?'

'In a manner of speaking. I gather from Celia that we're not the only client he's let down. And then there's the problem of his mother, and I think between you, me and the doorpost there may be other considerations too. But we can discuss all that later.'

Dougal noticed that his legs were trembling. 'Tomorrow,' he said.

'In half an hour.'

'But couldn't you get someone else?'

'No. Not in the circumstances. This could be rather important, couldn't it?' Hanbury paused, and the silence went on for far too long. 'Important in that Miles is handling the Custodemus account. You're uniquely qualified. Of course I don't—'

Hanbury's words were lost in a burst of static, which probably meant that he was using his car phone. Dougal held the handset away from his ears. The static stopped, and Hanbury's voice, diminished by the few inches between the handset and Dougal's ear, returned in full flow.

'—your actual client. Don't worry. I'll be there. I'll see you in Chiswick in about half an hour. Bye.'

The next fifty minutes passed in a painful blur. Dougal stood underneath the shower. He drank a pint of water and a mug of instant coffee. He swallowed three paracetamol. As he loaded his toothbrush with the toothpaste for sensitive teeth which he now required, he wondered with some bitterness how Hanbury managed to be so spry after an evening of such dissipation. Perhaps Joan Trotwood had miraculously rejuvenated him.

Eventually Dougal ran down a black plastic sack containing a clean if crumpled shirt. He put on a pair of cream trousers with irrevocably grass-stained knees and a baggy linen jacket which Celia said made him look like a failed rubber planter.

He decided to walk to Chiswick, partly in the hope that the exercise would clear his head a little more and partly to buy a paper. It was very hot outside. The heat made his bites itch. After a yard or two Dougal took off the jacket and carried it.

He passed a newsagent's and looked in at the window. He glimpsed his reflection and realized that he had forgotten to shave. Too late to do anything about that now.

The early edition of the *Standard* was on sale. He bought a copy and skimmed through it as he walked. The news was bad. SLOUGH FACTORY BLAZE. A police spokesman announced the discovery of human remains on the back seat of the gutted Ford Escort. The body had not yet been identified. The possibility of murder had not been ruled out. Enquiries were continuing.

But they were still quite safe, Dougal told himself. He had spent much of the last thirty-six hours going over the reasons why nothing could touch them. There was nothing to connect the charred remains with Miles Provender, not unless the police were tipped off, in which case dental records or genetic fingerprinting would probably allow a positive identification. But there wasn't going to be a tip-off. Even if there were, Dougal and Hanbury should still be safe. True, they had known Miles; but so had dozens, if not hundreds of people. No one had seen them with Miles. No one knew of any reason why they should wish to harm Miles. Even Celia had no idea that Dougal knew of her private relationship with him.

No, Dougal thought, as, sticky with sweat, he zigzagged among the shoppers on the Goldhawk Road, they were all right. He was going to get away with it. For once the gods were on his side and had been right from the start. Then for the first time he confronted the serendipity of it all. On Sunday evening events had acquired a dreamlike inevitability, but now there were questions to be asked and the lack of answers made Dougal feel queasy. How had Hanbury known about the conveniently parked Ford Escort at the empty factory? About the petrol in the car's tank, about the absence of witnesses? Had he planned to use them for another piece of private enterprise? Something to do with the toothsome Joan and Georgie Trotwood?

All too soon Dougal reached Brassard Prentisse's offices in a street off Chiswick High Road. Their suite was in a small block built in the boom years of the 1980s, a place of painted metal, smoked glass and grey marble. Dougal had not been here for several months. Since his last visit, the other two suites in the block had lost their tenants, victims perhaps of the recession.

Hanbury's Jaguar was already in the little car park. Dougal went into reception. He did not recognize the woman behind the desk. He identified himself and she gave him a token smile.

'I'm afraid the meeting's already begun, Mr Dougal. They're in Mr Brassard's room. Do you know where it is?'

The suite's layout was simple: most of the space was given to an open-plan area with the desks separated by low partitions. At the far end were half a dozen glassed-in offices. As Dougal walked towards the room in the far left-hand corner he noticed that several of the desks and at least one of the offices were apparently unused. All this was in stark contrast to his last visit when the Brassard Prentisse Christmas party had been in full swing and the place had been packed with people getting drunk and making desperate jokes about the recession. Hugo Brassard, suffering from what had been eventually diagnosed as a bad case of salmonella, had left early in an ambulance. But what Dougal most remembered about the occasion was that first meeting with Miles.

'Hello,' Miles had said, swanning across the office as if he owned the place. 'I don't think we've met. I'm Miles Provender.' He had looked Dougal straight in the eye and engulfed his hand with the regulation vicelike grip. 'Are you a client or press?'

Dougal pushed the memory into the back of his mind. He saw movement in Brassard's office. Celia and Hanbury were sitting side by side on the sofa. Dougal was relieved to see that there was no one in the room who could possibly be Miles's mother. As he drew nearer the door opened and Brassard appeared. He ran thin fingers through his wiry hair. He was almost dancing with agitation.

'William – where've you been?'

The phone began to ring behind him. Brassard moaned. He darted to his desk and seized the handset.

'I thought I said—' he began. He stopped abruptly and grimaced at Celia. 'No – of course, fine: put her on.'

Dougal came into the room and shut the door behind him. Hanbury nodded; Celia smiled and waved him to an armchair facing the sofa across a coffee table. On the table in front of Celia was a road atlas and a shorthand notepad.

'No, indeed,' Brassard said into the phone, in a rich, obsequious voice which had lost all trace of its previous agitation. 'We are actually in conference at this very moment with . . . Two private investigators, actually, people with the highest . . . No, he *is* the head of the firm . . . As you say . . . I'll tell them . . . No trouble at all, the personal touch is . . . I'll report as soon as there's news . . . Thank you so much for calling . . . Goodbye.'

He put down the phone, scowled and sat down behind his desk.

'That's the fifth time today,' Celia said, taking off her glasses and rubbing her eyes.

'And it won't be the last,' Brassard said. 'You can bank on that.'

Celia turned to Dougal. 'Thank you for coming at such short notice.'

Dougal felt like a plumber who did not usually operate a twenty-four-hour service. Hanbury took out his cigarettes and lit a Caporal. Brassard leapt up with an ashtray, which he placed on the coffee table. It was a large and approximately circular piece of pottery, glazed green. Around its wavering rim a legend was incised in drunken yellow capitals: FOR UNCLE HUGO WITH LOVE FROM CHARLOTTE.

'I wonder – would you like me to bring William up to date?' Hanbury asked.

'Please do.' Brassard opened a window and sank down behind his desk. His body was short and small but his arms and legs were very long. He put his elbows on the desk and his head between his hands. His eyes peered through the bars of his fingers.

Hanbury smiled at Celia. 'All right with you?' When she nodded, he turned to Dougal. 'You've met Miles, of course?'

'Two or three times. Briefly.'

'To the best of our knowledge he was last seen on Saturday afternoon. Playing golf in Twickenham with a client.'

'Typical,' Brassard said. 'He's very hard-working. That's what counts in this job, how you use the anti-social hours. That's what sorts the men from the boys.'

Hanbury smoothly regained the initiative: 'Hugo's contacted the client, of course, man called Forster, and he said Miles seemed perfectly normal and promised he'd be in touch on Monday. Quite urgent, too – about the arrangements for a product launch. But Miles didn't come into work on Monday. Hugo tried to phone him at home, but all he got was the answering machine.'

'It was very odd,' Brassard interrupted again. 'Miles is very conscientious. And it wasn't as if yesterday was going to be a slack day. Quite apart from his own work he was covering for Celia.'

'Quite so,' Hanbury said, and Dougal guessed that he was not best pleased at the interruptions. 'As I was saying, Hugo then phoned Celia to see if she knew where he was. She didn't, of course' – Hanbury gave her a courtly smile – 'but she felt that in the circumstances she had better cut short her holiday.'

Naturally, Dougal thought, surreptitiously scratching one of his bites: her worry about Miles would have outweighed her concern for Eleanor's welfare and the potential embarrassment of seeing Eleanor's father.

'I'd have had to come back early in any case,' Celia said, as though defending herself from Dougal's unspoken accusation. 'Something else has come up. I've got a meeting with a client this afternoon.'

'Yes,' Brassard said, looking up, his eyes bright. 'You were going to tell me about that.'

'Later.' Celia spoke to the space between Dougal and Hanbury: 'All this is so unlike Miles. He's a very punctual and responsible person.'

'Where does he live?' Dougal asked. 'Has anyone been round there?'

'Richmond,' Celia said. 'I went there yesterday evening. His car's there. He wasn't answering the door.'

She looked so tired and dispirited that for an instant Dougal felt angry with Miles for inflicting the burden of his disappearance on her.

'So,' Hanbury said, stubbing out his cigarette in the lurid ashtray. 'Miles vanishes. Exit Miles – and enter Miles's mother.'

'She started phoning yesterday afternoon,' Brassard said. 'She had a dream, you see. She's a great one for omens. She dreamed that Miles was in a fix, that he needed her. Though personally I'd say it was more like the other way round.'

'Mrs Provender is a woman of determination,' Hanbury said. 'She phoned Celia as well. And the police. And every hospital she could think of. No luck, of course. As you know, the police can be less than helpful in these cases. Miles is over eighteen and there's nothing to suggest that anything criminal has occurred. So Mrs Provender has put the matter in Celia's and Hugo's hands.'

'Why you?' Dougal said suddenly, looking not at Celia but at Brassard. 'I mean, you're not responsible for Miles.'

Brassard rubbed his eyes with his knuckles. 'There are reasons why we would like to co-operate in every possible way with Mrs Provender.'

There was a pause, which soon became awkward. No one deigned to explain the reasons to Dougal.

'Quite so,' Hanbury said at last, to no one in particular. He went on, addressing Dougal: 'Hugo and Celia have advised Mrs Provender to retain a private investigator.'

'So convenient,' Brassard said. 'What with Custodemus being a client, and your both knowing Miles.'

'Keep it in the family, as it were,' Hanbury remarked.

Dougal looked up and caught Celia's eyes on him. He said to Hanbury, 'So are we working directly for Mrs Provender?'

'It's not quite as simple as that. She is our client and she will of course have the final say. But I gather that she wants Brassard Prentisse to have an active interest in the investigation: to act as her agents.'

'Which makes perfect sense in the circumstances,' Brassard said. 'Doesn't it, Celia?'

'Our priority,' Hanbury said, 'must be to search Miles's flat.'

'Mrs Provender has a spare set of keys,' Celia said.

'Does she want to be there herself?' Dougal asked.

'No, she can't.'

Dougal felt enormous relief. 'We could send a bike for the keys,' he suggested. 'No point in wasting time.'

'Actually, no.' Brassard smiled apologetically. 'Mrs Provender is very keen to brief you in person. She likes the personal touch.'

She who pays the piper calls the tune. Dougal wriggled in the armchair, which was too low for comfort.

'I'd come myself,' Hanbury said. 'Unfortunately I've got a meeting after lunch.'

'She wanted one of us to come with you,' Brassard said, hunching himself over his desk. 'But it's quite out of the question. We're up to our ears in work.'

'That must be very gratifying for you,' Hanbury said, 'given the current economic climate.'

Dougal glanced sharply at him. He wondered if he had imagined the throwaway malice in Hanbury's voice.

'I hope you don't mind my mentioning it,' Brassard said to Dougal, 'but would you possibly be able to shave before you go down?'

'Come off it, Hugo,' Celia snapped. 'What does it matter?'

'It's just that one doesn't want to create a bad impression. Some people are so foolish about that sort of thing.'

'Yes, indeed,' said Hanbury.

'We could lend you an electric razor,' Brassard went on, his face twitching. 'Miles has got one, hasn't he, Celia? I'm sure he wouldn't mind your borrowing it. Not in the circumstances.'

Celia shrugged. 'I think we should warn William. The Provenders are—'

At that moment the door opened unexpectedly. A young girl stood on the threshold. Brassard looked up and suddenly his face filled with warmth. For an instant the emotion transfigured him. It was as if a light had come on in the room behind a curtained window.

'Charlotte, I am so sorry. I quite forgot.'

The girl blushed. She had the pale, freckled skin that flushes with cruel ease. She wore long shorts, sandals and a baggy white T-shirt. Her curly hair was an unusual shade of dark red; she wore it tied back. Her eyes were large and panic-stricken behind her glasses.

'We were going to have lunch, weren't we? I'm afraid we'll have to postpone it.'

'How are you?' Celia said. 'Eleanor's still talking about your picnic in Kew Gardens.'

Charlotte smiled. 'How is she?'

'Very well. She's staying with her granny for a few days.'

Brassard got up and came towards his niece. If he had been a hen he would have clucked. Charlotte ducked her head, as if embarrassed by his concern. By chance her eyes met Dougal's. She looked straight through him, though they had met twice before, albeit briefly, once at the Christmas party and once at Kew.

'We're at sixes and sevens today,' Brassard said. 'Bit of a problem, you see. We've mislaid Miles.'

'Miles . . .?'

'You know Miles. Chap in the room between Celia's and mine.'

'Oh yes.'

'Well, he didn't turn up yesterday, or today, which means lots of work for the rest of us. Never mind, we'll cope.' Brassard ushered her out of the room. 'Let's see if we can get you a taxi.'

'Poor old Hugo,' Hanbury murmured. 'He doesn't seem to know whether he's coming or going.'

'I don't think any of us does,' Celia said.

'It's a difficult time for everyone, isn't it?' Hanbury glanced at Celia and went on: 'I don't think I've met Charlotte.'

'Hugo's niece.'

'Of course.' He tapped the ashtray. 'Uncle Hugo. And a friend of your daughter's, too?'

'Charlotte did some child-minding for me once. But I felt she was a bit young for the responsibility.' She turned to Dougal, who rapidly suppressed the bitterness he felt at Celia's choice of pronouns. 'I'd better show you where the Provenders live.'

She leaned forward and picked up the road atlas. The movement dislodged the shorthand notepad, which fell to the floor. Dougal picked it up. The pad was open. Celia had scribbled a few words on the top sheet: *A1 to Biggleswade. B1040 to Stanford. Then follow signs.*

Celia leafed through the road atlas. 'It's quite tricky, I'm afraid.'

Dougal thought that of course she would know the route well. No doubt Miles had taken her to meet his parents.

'It's a village called Thricehurst,' Celia said, and a strand of her hair touched Dougal's arm. 'Look, it's there.'

Just then Brassard returned alone. 'Sorry about that.' He handed Dougal a desk diary. 'It's Miles's. I thought you might want to see it. Go on, have a look.'

Celia sighed, almost inaudibly. Dougal sensed her irritation. He opened the diary at random and found a page full of appointments.

'He probably spends more time on the road than in the office,' Brassard said. 'These days we have to go where the work is. I hardly saw him last week. He spent Wednesday in Leeds, and Thursday in Bournemouth. Which reminds me – I suppose you'll be checking all his professional contacts?'

'Yes, of course,' Dougal said.

'I'll see you get a list. But do tread carefully, won't you? We don't want to give the wrong impression. It's bad enough that—'

Celia interrupted: 'Could we discuss this later? I was just showing William where Thricehurst is. And I think we should tell him about Mr and Mrs Provender.'

Brassard's face became wary. 'By all means. If you're not expecting—'

'Not just that,' Celia said. 'Why they're important to us.'

'Is that strictly necessary?'

She ignored his question. 'And we should tell him why Miles is important, too.'

Dougal looked up from the diary. 'Please do,' he said.

55

6

Mr Stanley Provender's mouth was open. He was sitting in an imposing leather armchair in his study. He wore a dressing gown and red-and-white striped pyjamas. His feet were bare because he had kicked off his leather slippers, and his toenails needed cutting. In his hand was an unlit briar pipe with a much chewed, curly stem.

When he caught sight of Dougal standing in the doorway, he smiled and burst into song.

'Oh, my darling, oh my darling, oh my darling Clementine!' he sang. 'Thou art lost and gone for ever, dreadful sorry, Clementine.'

As he sang he conducted himself with the pipe. He was a big man with a heavy chin and high cheekbones. He looked like a personable version of an Easter Island statue. There was an air of effortless competence about him, as if in his time he had captained both cricket teams and industries with equal efficiency. He repeated the verse twice and then simpered at Dougal, who realized that Mr Provender was awaiting applause.

'Very nice,' Dougal said.

Stanley Provender subsided in his chair. Slowly his face lost its animation. His attention drifted away from his audience. His skin was lined and chalky; it looked very soft.

The room smelled of talcum powder and polish, and more faintly of urine and disinfectant. There was a set of hunting prints in gilt frames on the wall and a trophy in the shape of a golf ball in the centre of the mantelpiece. Behind the door was a walking frame, a wheelchair, a set of golf clubs and a commode. A bookcase contained well-thumbed Wisdens and a selection of adventure thrillers in paperback editions. On top of the bookcase was a row of photographs, most of which were of Miles. One of the few exceptions showed Mr Provender, looking very commanding in a dinner jacket, shaking hands with a member of the royal family.

'Aargh,' gargled Stanley Provender, returning from wherever he had been. 'Aargh. Aargh.'

'Um,' said Dougal in what he hoped was a reassuring manner. 'Um.'

The two armchairs and the sofa were covered with green leather, as was the top of the large desk. A pair of antlers hung above the fireplace above a fish in a glass case. Even the waste-paper basket looked as if it had once been attached to an elephant. How many creatures great and small, Dougal wondered, had made involuntary contributions to the furniture?

'Aargh,' said Mr Provender again.

'That's quite enough of that, Stanley,' said a voice behind Dougal. 'Stop showing off.'

Dougal turned, smiling. 'Mrs Provender?'

She was a bulky, stooping woman in her sixties with tightly permed grey hair. She wore a faded, coral-coloured sweatshirt and dark green slacks which emphasized her long, heavy haunches.

'Yes? And who are you?'

'My name's William Dougal. From Custodemus.' He took a card from the top pocket of his jacket and gave it to her. 'I believe you're expecting me.'

'Not as early as this.' She studied the card. *CUSTODEMUS – Permanent Peace of Mind.*

'The traffic was easier than I thought it would be. Look – I'm sorry to barge in. I met a woman coming out—'

'She cleans. Or says she does.'

'—and she said to ring the bell and come in.' He guessed that Mrs Provender had been in the lavatory or in the garden.

'Well, it doesn't matter. We'll have tea. Come along.'

'Yum,' said Mr Provender with an air of desperation. 'Yum. Yum.'

'Don't worry,' his wife said with a hint of irritation. 'We'll have it here. Just be patient for once, will you?'

His head flopped forward on to his chest. He dropped the pipe on his lap. His hands lay palm downwards on his thighs and precisely aligned with his legs.

'They had the sense to warn you?' Mrs Provender asked Dougal.

'Yes.'

She sniffed. 'Come along. You can give me a hand.'

Dougal followed her down a broad, panelled hall, painted pale yellow, into a kitchen whose bright and ultra-modern fittings contrasted sharply with what he had seen of the rest of the house.

'There's a nurse who helps with the evenings and the nights,' Mrs Provender shouted over the roar of water gushing into the kettle. 'And other people come and go in the day. But he doesn't feel comfortable with them.' She plugged in the kettle, put her hands on her hips and turned to face Dougal. 'He pines if I'm not there. Like a dog. If I'm gone for more than about an hour, he gets very upset. Funny, isn't it?'

'Not really,' Dougal said.

She looked sharply at him. 'And if I'm not there he worries about not getting his biscuit. Also like a dog, come to think of it. He always was greedy about food. Liked his grub. So you had a good drive down?'

The change of subject caught Dougal off balance. He managed to mutter something about wishing he had caught the train. Mrs Provender remarked that Thricehurst was very fortunate to have its own station; British Rail had spared it because the village was on one of the main commuter routes of the south-east.

While she made the tea, Mrs Provender held the conversation on a straight course through an unruffled sea of banalities. Their theme was transport. When the railway was exhausted, they discussed parking in Tunbridge Wells, how the motor car had ruined Sussex and the pros and cons of the Channel Tunnel (chiefly the cons).

'Not that I get out much at present,' Mrs Provender said. 'My husband finds it unsettling to be away from home.'

In its way, Dougal thought, it was a practised performance: Mrs Provender was clearly used to conversing decorously, if tediously, with unattached males younger than herself; and Dougal, too, could play the undemanding role she had allotted him with distinction. The great advantage of such conversations was that they left most of the mind free: while they talked, Dougal studied his hostess and his surroundings; and he had no doubt that Mrs Provender was studying him.

Among other things he thought about the house – older and larger than its narrow eighteenth-century brick frontage suggested, and set in a secluded cul-de-sac in the heart of this almost monotonously picturesque village.

What he had seen of the contents murmured of money. Everything looked nearly new, expensive and built to last. Colours and patterns matched. The furniture in the study and the hall had been chosen to occupy the spaces they now filled. This was a home for people who intended to lead structured lives, a house co-ordinated and carefully planned; the result was almost certainly a credit to one or two of the better London department stores. It made Dougal acutely conscious of the messiness of his own home, such as it was, and his own life.

Simultaneously Dougal found this evidence of the Provenders' forethought deeply depressing for another reason. Such organization, such effort, such a passion for order, such outpourings of time and money – and where had they led? To uncut toenails and 'Clementine'.

Mrs Provender laid the tray with Portmeirion china – apart from a plastic beaker with two handles and a lid for Mr Provender. There was a plate containing six expensive biscuits, the sort which come wrapped in determinedly archaic packaging. Dougal picked up the tray.

'Try and keep your voice down,' Mrs Provender said. 'Otherwise the old boy gets upset. Funny, eh? I think someone must have shouted at him a long time ago.'

Nothing had changed in the study apart from the line of dribble which now ran like a snail track from the corner of Mr Provender's mouth. The sight of it reminded Dougal of the convoy of snails crossing Celia's garden path, and how their shells had crunched and cracked as he had dragged Miles's body towards the gate.

Mrs Provender told him to put the tray on the desk and mopped up the dribble with a paper handkerchief. She directed Dougal to an armchair beside the open window. Breathing heavily, she poured the tea with brisk efficiency and handed round the biscuits.

Outside the window was a terrace with weathered stone flags and two reclining wooden seats. The garden was long and colourful, though verging on the unkempt. It was bounded by old brick walls. In the distance was the tower of the parish church, but no other houses were visible.

Mr Provender ate two biscuits very quickly. He coughed because a crumb went down the wrong way, and Mrs Provender had to pat his back. Then she perched on the arm of his chair and gave him sips of tea from his beaker.

'Oh, my darling,' Mr Provender sang softly between sips, 'oh my darling.'

'Hush now,' said Mrs Provender, sounding curiously flustered. 'Would you like another biscuit?' When her husband had finished, she stayed on the arm of the chair. She said to Dougal, 'Hugo Brassard says you know Miles?'

'I've met him,' Dougal said. 'I wouldn't exactly say I know him.'

Mrs Provender smiled unexpectedly. 'Still, it makes it easier for me. And perhaps it'll help you to understand why all this is so much odder than it seems.'

'In what way?'

'Because of the sort of person Miles is.' She picked a crumb from one thigh of her slacks and deposited it on her saucer.

'He's our only child,' she went on abruptly. 'He arrived when we'd more or less given up hoping. So often the way, isn't it? So we were rather older than most of his friends' parents. I don't know if that had anything to do with it.'

She fell silent. Her hand picked up her husband's. Dougal waited.

'You see, even when he was quite young it was as if he was looking after us as much as we were looking after him. He's always felt responsible for us. Oh dear – am I making sense?'

'Yum,' said Mr Provender. 'Yummy.'

His wife picked up the last of the biscuits and began to feed it to him.

Dougal said, 'You mean, he's not the sort of person to go off somewhere without telling you?'

Mrs Provender looked up and nodded. For an instant Dougal thought he read terror in her eyes. She wasn't a fool. She knew that if she was right about her estimate of her son's character, then something drastic must have happened to prevent him from being in touch.

'Since he's left home he's always been very good about telephoning. Especially in the last few years.' Her eyes strayed back to her husband, who was contentedly munching the last of the biscuit. 'Not quite every day but very nearly. Certainly every other day.'

'When did you last talk to him?'

'Saturday evening. He just phoned to say hello, really – it wasn't a long call, and I did most of the talking.'

'Nothing out of the ordinary?'

'No.'

'Did he mention any plans he had for Sunday or Monday?'

She shook her head. 'There's a gym he sometimes goes to on Sundays. I don't know where it is. Or he might have been meeting friends. He's got lots of friends.'

'Perhaps we can find his address book. It's possible that there's a perfectly natural and harmless explanation. Perhaps he met someone.'

She was there almost before Dougal. 'A girl, you mean? Swept off his feet? But Miles isn't like that. He's careful, thoughtful. He's never been the type for sudden infatuations.'

Dougal wondered how she could be so certain. Sudden infatuations might be just the thing you would conceal from your doting mother.

'And even if he were,' she went on, 'I'm sure he'd find time to phone his old mum.'

'Did you try phoning him on Sunday?'

'No, not till Monday. It was partly because of the last episode of *Inspector Coleford* and partly because of the dream.'

'I don't follow.'

'I had friends coming round on Monday evening so I wanted to set the video to record it. I've never been able to make head or tail of the manual. They're always worse than useless, those things, might as well be written in Japanese; or perhaps it's me. Still, when I want to set the timer on the video, I always ask Miles, and he tells me what to do. He's so good with machines.'

'So you phoned the office – when?'

'I don't know. Before lunch sometime. They said he hadn't come in, so I phoned the flat. I got the answering machine. He usually leaves it on if he's going out for any length of time. Just in case . . . just in case there's something urgent.' She nibbled her lower lip. 'So that's why I was so worried. That and the dream.'

'This was a dream you had on Sunday night?'

'I can't remember much about it. It was about Miles needing me. I got the impression he was desperate. He had his hands stretched out . . . Do you take notice of your dreams?'

'Not very often.'

'You should. I find they tell you things. Anyway, they're fascinating in themselves.'

Dougal nodded politely. He found most of his dreams rather boring. Either they were rubbish, the debris left over from his waking life, or they dramatized, usually without much subtlety or narrative thrust, his mood of the moment. Given a choice, he would much prefer to watch *Inspector Coleford*.

Mrs Provender got up from the arm of the chair and picked up the teapot. Suddenly she developed a powerful curiosity about the practicalities of what Dougal would do. He wondered if she wanted to divert attention from what she had been saying.

Dougal described the standard Custodemus procedure for a missing-persons investigation. Like most of Custodemus's work there was nothing arcane about it; it boiled down to teamwork, perseverance, a good telephone manner and attention to detail. And in this case, which was being co-ordinated by Hanbury himself, there could be no short cuts. The procedure would be followed to the last tedious particular – partly because of Dougal's special relationship with Miles and partly because there were so many interested parties.

Dougal had assumed that he had killed a single person with three taps of a hammer. Now it seemed that Miles had been not one person but several. Everyone who had known him, including Dougal himself, had his or her own version of Miles. The dead Miles was revealing himself as an infinitely more complicated proposition than the living one had been.

'In a sense,' Hugo Brassard had said towards the end of the briefing this morning, 'Miles is rather more than a promising account executive. He's also a potential partner who could bring us a substantial injection of capital.'

Dougal had watched Celia's face and thought how pale and weary it was. He had wished he could bring Miles back to life just to make her happy.

Now in Mr Provender's study, Mrs Provender was saying something; and her voice sounded irritated.

'I'm sorry,' Dougal said. 'I missed that.'

Mrs Provender frowned. 'I said you'll need a photograph.'

Involuntarily they both glanced at the row of frames on the bookcase. Miles as a baby, a boy, a teenager, an adult.

'Not one of those. There's some more here.'

Mrs Provender opened one of the desk drawers and took out a pile of prints – perhaps fifty of them, colour and black-and-white, and in a variety of formats. She stood over Dougal as he leafed through them. It was even worse than Dougal had feared, this exposure to Miles as a son. Among them there was Miles in a pushchair; a boyish Miles in a team photograph; Miles with a cricket bat; Miles with a rugby ball; a professional shot of Miles in a suit at a product launch with both Brassard and Celia hovering in the background. He had photographed well, too.

Dougal chose the publicity shot and an obviously recent passport-sized photograph.

Mrs Provender took the discarded photographs and flicked through them herself. She was breathing even more heavily than before. 'He's a good-looking boy, isn't he? Everyone says so.'

Suddenly and unexpectedly, Dougal felt a wave of sympathy towards Miles. Had his parents never let him go? Had they bound him to them with pity and money now that their need for him was greater than his for them?

'You'll take great care of them, won't you?' Mrs Provender said.

'If you like I can have them copied and send you back the originals.'

'That would be so kind. You must let me know what it costs. Which reminds me – we must have a chat about money, mustn't we? I must give you something to be going on with.'

Custodemus's company policy emphasized the importance of extracting money from clients as soon as possible. But there were occasional exceptions where a more diplomatic approach to the question of remuneration was encouraged. Hanbury had delicately intimated to Dougal that Mrs Provender came into this category. There had been no need for him to spell out his thinking: it wasn't worth running the risk of Mrs Provender choosing another firm just for the sake of a few hundred pounds.

'I'm not going to be counting the pennies,' Mrs Provender said. 'I want Miles: that's what counts.'

A lot of clients said that they didn't mind what it cost, and they meant it too; and then when the case was sorted out and you presented the final bill, they quibbled about every item.

'But I do want you to keep in touch. That's the one thing I insist on – a phone call once a day, just to report what you've been doing. And you must phone in any case if you have any real news.' She paused, then added, 'Good or bad, and at any time of the day or night. One likes to know the truth.'

'Yes,' Dougal said. 'One does.' But in this case he devoutly hoped that one of them wasn't going to get it.

Mrs Provender glanced dourly at him, perhaps wondering if he were mocking her. She laid the photographs on the desk.

'Aargh,' said her husband, looking excited. He held out his hands.

'You want to see them too? Of course you may.'

She gave Mr Provender the prints. Dougal watched her wincing as the clumsy fingers creased and smudged the photographs; but she said nothing.

'Miles,' said Mr Provender in a deep, manly voice. 'Miles.'

'Yes, darling.'

Dougal stood up. She opened another drawer in the desk and took out two keys on a ring. They looked identical to the keys he had taken from Miles's pocket. She gave them to him.

'For the flat?' he asked.

She nodded. 'You have the address?'

'Celia Prentisse gave it to me.'

'Ah. Celia.' Mrs Provender lingered on the name.

Dougal, sensing the approach of a possible question about his relationship with Celia, rushed in with a diversion: 'Do you always have a set of keys for Miles's flat?'

'Oh yes. Now you won't disturb anything will you? Miles gets so cross if people fiddle around with his things. Tell me, what will you actually do? Look for clues or something like Inspector Coleford?'

'Not quite like that.' Dougal enjoyed watching Inspector Coleford in action: the inspector's principal talents as a detective were his intuition, which verged on the paranormal, and his astonishing ability to be in the right place at the right time.

'I'll see if his toothbrush is there. His credit cards. Check the answering machine.'

Mrs Provender was moving towards the door. 'Talking of machines, you wouldn't mind having a look at the video while I write you a cheque? The clock seems to think it's still Sunday.'

'I can try,' Dougal said.

'Miles?' Mr Provender said. 'Where's Miles?'

Miles is miles away, Dougal thought.

'Ah – there's Miles,' said Mr Provender, looking at Dougal. 'See?'

'Don't be silly, darling.'

Dougal followed Mrs Provender into a large, square drawing room decorated in pastel shades. She sat at a reproduction Queen Anne bureau to write the cheque while he crouched down and tinkered with the video, which was concealed in a Regency-style cabinet. Even Dougal, who conspicuously lacked Miles's aptitude for machines, found it easy to set the clock to the right time.

He straightened up. Mrs Provender was still at the bureau. She was looking fixedly at him.

'Seems OK now,' Dougal said awkwardly.

'I hope so.'

She held out the cheque. Automatically Dougal glanced at it as he put it away in his wallet. He noticed two things. First, she had doubled the amount of the deposit which he had suggested. Second, her Christian name was Clementine.

7

Dougal wasn't expecting trouble. There was no reason to do so, none in the world. After all, Miles was dead.

The flat was on the top floor of a low, purpose-built block within earshot of Richmond Station and Sheen Road. The building had a communal garden at the front, whose trees looked older than the flats themselves. The drive gave on to a residential street which was also a through route. At the back was another, smaller street, too close for comfort to the railway.

It was only just half past seven by the time Dougal got there. He was on foot. He had left his car near the station and taken a half-hour break for a pizza and a cup of coffee. He lingered over the meal but he was still a quarter of an hour early.

The evening was warm and bright; the weather showed no signs of breaking. Dougal walked through the garden towards a car park for residents. One of the cars it contained was a purple Vauxhall Cavalier, presumably Miles's. There were several other cars but Dougal was not surprised by the absence of Hanbury's.

He moved slowly towards the flats. The block was faced with damp-stained concrete relieved by horizontal bands of dark grey pebbledash. Televisions chattered through open windows hung with net curtains. There was no other sign of life.

Swing-doors led to a hallway with a concrete floor and brick walls decorated with the occasional fire extinguisher. There were twelve flats, four to each floor. Dougal wanted number nine. He began to climb the stairs, which were made of concrete with iron handrails.

He met no one. On the top landing there were four red

doors, each with a spyhole. Dougal rang the bell of Miles's flat. If he was being observed by a neighbour, and if he was ever challenged about his actions, ringing the bell would seem a perfectly natural thing to do. The open-minded private investigator would allow for the possibility that Miles had returned. There was also a slim chance that Hanbury might have got here early; he could have used the keys they had taken from Miles to let himself in.

While Dougal waited he took out the keys which Mrs Provender had given him. There were two – a Yale and a five-lever Chubb. When no one answered the door he simply assumed Hanbury hadn't arrived.

Dougal pushed the Chubb key into the lock. It wouldn't turn. He tried twice more. Puzzled, he reversed the movement and turned in a clockwise direction. The lock shot home into the jamb.

Even then he wasn't suspicious. He was tired, of course, and a little depressed; but most of all he had no reason to anticipate any problems. The only real criminal involved in this business was Dougal himself. So he hardly bothered to think about the implications. It was remotely possible that Hanbury had already come and gone. Or, much more likely, Miles had simply forgotten to turn the Chubb when he left the flat on Sunday evening. People could be astonishingly careless.

Dougal unlocked the Chubb and pushed the Yale key into its lock. It turned easily. He opened the door, pocketed the keys, slipped inside and shut the door behind him.

For a few seconds he stood there on the mat. The hall was small and rectangular. Three interior doors opened into it. All of them were slightly ajar. In the corner between two of the doors was a little table on which stood the answering machine and a die-cast model of a red Ferrari.

He stooped and picked up the letters – a Barclaycard bill, a circular advertising a prize draw and a few words scrawled on a page torn from a shorthand notebook.

Monday 6.30 p.m.: Miles – Please ring me, home or office – Celia.

Hanbury's absence was a relief. Dougal wanted a little time to get used to Miles's flat. It struck him that when you killed a person, you destroyed a great deal more than a single human being. You destroyed parts of other people – your victim's family, friends and other social contacts; you left your victim's possessions bereft of their owner.

At least there were no widows and orphans in this case – not unless one counted Celia. Dougal sniffed. He thought there was perfume in the air. Was it Celia's? Suddenly he was scared of what he might find.

He barged through the door on his left and found himself in a small living room. The curtains were half drawn. The window faced west. A yellow stripe of evening sunlight stretched across the floor. The air was hot and stuffy, and he thought there was a hint of the same perfume.

Miles had kept the furniture to a minimum – a long low sofa, a modern pine table with four folding chairs and a large, grid-like shelving unit. On the shelves were a small, expensive stereo system, a television, a video, CDs and tapes, three black box files, a couple of lamps, and a model of a red Porsche. The walls were decorated with pictures of motorbikes – large, gleaming machines, some of which had large, gleaming blondes astride them. The carpet was grey. There was an Indian rug in front of the sofa. In the far corner of the room was another door.

Dougal felt irrationally hostile towards Miles's innocuous possessions. How could anyone surround himself with such nasty objects? Then he realized his own arrogance, and found it equally distasteful.

'Sorry, Miles,' he whispered.

Dougal crossed the room. The CDs offered a selection of bubblegum music. One of the tapes was a pre-recorded video from the last series of *Inspector Coleford*.

The door in the corner led to a galley kitchen. It was very tidy apart from the sink, in which stood a cafetière, a mug and a couple of plates. The last supper, Dougal thought. Curious to know what Miles had eaten, he opened the refrigerator door. Inside was an array of food and drink from Marks & Spencer. The carrier bag which Miles had worn on his last journey had been more appropriate than Dougal had realized.

Just as he was thinking this he heard running feet. It took him a few vital seconds to decide that the sounds came from Miles's flat, not from a neighbouring one. A door slammed – a heavy door because the vibration it caused reached the kitchen. Dougal ran into the living room. His left foot hooked itself around one of the folding chairs leaning against the wall. He fell inelegantly on the floor. He scrambled up and went into the hall.

The door opposite him had been a few inches ajar. Now it was wide open. Dougal could see the corner of a bed and a dark blue duvet. He tried the front door. In his haste he thought it must have jammed. He wasted more precious seconds trying to tug it open. At last he realized that the Chubb had been locked, presumably from the outside. He fumbled for his set of keys, eventually finding them in the last of the five possible pockets.

By now he knew it was too late. He opened the door and listened. Whoever it had been was long gone. He glanced inside the bedroom and the bathroom. There was no sign of disturbance. He went back into the living room, pulled aside the curtains and stared down at the communal garden. Nothing moved, not even a cat.

Dougal stood at the living-room window for more than a minute. At first he damned his own stupidity – he should have given the whole flat a quick check as soon as he had got there; instead he had mooned around like a man in a dream. But if he were to be honest with himself, he couldn't ignore the relief he felt. His mismanagement of the situation had at least avoided the need for a direct confrontation.

The relief was short-lived. In its turn it was pushed aside by another emotion, anxiety. Miles's life had produced yet another posthumous surprise. And this one might be dangerous.

The presence of the intruder was like the unexpected appearance of a joker in a game of rummy: it forced you to modify all previous calculations. Whoever it was had seen the contents of the flat before Dougal and Hanbury. Whoever it was might have known Miles sufficiently well for him to mention where he was going on Sunday evening.

The worries squirmed inside him like a nest of snakes. Someone had a third set of keys. Clementine Provender? Had she suddenly realized that there would be something embarrassing among her son's possessions, something she wouldn't want a stranger to see? It seemed unlikely she would not have thought of it before, and even more unlikely that she would have two sets of keys.

Celia was a much more plausible possibility. If she and Miles were lovers, of course she would have had keys for the flat: they would have had to meet here because Dougal and Eleanor had been at the Kew house. Perhaps she had left something in the bedroom, something which revealed the intimate nature of her relationship with Miles. She wouldn't have removed it last night when she left the message for Miles because at that stage she wouldn't have known that Miles was really missing and that Mrs Provender was going to send Dougal round to the flat.

The explanation had a dreadful logic. The theory was all the more convincing because Dougal didn't want to believe it; even thinking about it was painful. This, he thought, is part of the punishment.

A movement below him caught his attention. A black Jaguar turned into the access road and rolled slowly through the garden, past the garages and into the visitors' car park. It nosed its way into the parking space beside the Vauxhall Cavalier.

Hanbury got out of the car. He was wearing dark glasses and a blazer with a crest on the front pocket. It seemed to Dougal that he glanced up at the windows of Miles's flat. Dougal automatically took a step backwards: observers do not like to be observed. Hanbury walked quickly towards the flats.

Another idea about the intruder occurred to Dougal – as worrying as the Celia theory, though for a very different reason. Hanbury had taken charge of Miles's set of keys on Sunday evening. Hanbury had known when Dougal was planning to visit the flat because Dougal had telephoned him from Thricehurst and arranged to meet him here at seven forty-five. As a corollary, Hanbury had every reason to expect that the flat would be empty at seven-thirty.

But why should Hanbury of all people want to pay a preemptive visit to Miles Provender's flat?

Hanbury edged past Dougal into the hall. There was a tiny smudge of lipstick on his cheek. Suddenly the hall shrank. Hanbury was a big man and all the interior doors were shut. Dougal closed the door to the landing and the hall became even more claustrophobic, more like a prison cell. He wanted to run away to a land full of wide open spaces.

'Am I late?' Hanbury asked.

'I was early.'

'It took me a while to find this place. Had to ask a policeman in the end.' Hanbury smiled. 'Useful practice.'

'What?'

'There's probably going to be a new royal commission on law and order. In which case I may be asking policemen at all levels a great many – ah – pertinent questions.'

'You?' Dougal said. 'On a royal commission? Are you sure?'

'Perfectly sure, thank you,' Hanbury said frostily. 'I'm meeting Charlie Jones on Thursday for a preliminary chat.'

'Who's he?'

Hanbury sighed. 'He's a minister of state at the Home Office. So have you been here long?'

'Five minutes, maybe.'

'What have you come up with?'

'Nothing yet.' Dougal hesitated. If Hanbury had been the intruder, he would know that Dougal must have been aware of his departure; and if he hadn't been the intruder he was a potential ally. 'There was someone in the flat when I arrived. They must have been in the bedroom. As soon as I came in here they rushed off.'

Hanbury swung round, his expression both puzzled and surprised. He glanced from Dougal to the door of the bedroom. 'Did you see him?'

It was perfectly done. Dougal would have been quite convinced if he hadn't known how capably Hanbury could act a part.

'I heard them,' Dougal said. 'Whoever it was had a key. They locked me in.'

'Oh dear. How disturbing.'

'Can you smell perfume?'

Hanbury sniffed. 'Aftershave, I'd say. Very faint – it's probably Miles's.' He opened the living-room door. 'Come on, let's get this over with.' On the threshold he paused and surveyed the room. 'Good God. How ghastly.'

'Not ghastly,' Dougal said. 'Adolescent. It's as if part of him never got beyond sixteen.'

Hanbury wandered across to the shelves and took out one of the box files. He put it on the table and opened it. 'There's not a great deal we can do, is there? Except carry on as planned.'

Dougal watched as Hanbury put on a pair of reading glasses and tipped the file's contents on to the table: bank statements, a building society passbook, documents relating to insurance and pensions.

'There's a lot we don't know about Master Miles,' Hanbury observed, glancing over the glasses at Dougal. 'We've got a job to do, and of course an ethical duty to our client.'

Dougal blinked. What was Hanbury afraid of? Mrs Provender lurking behind the sofa?

'Of course we're duty-bound to pass on any relevant information,' Hanbury went on. 'But we must also be prepared to use our discretion with material which isn't – ah – germane to the enquiry. Few of us would want to be entirely frank with our mothers, and I'm sure Miles is no exception.'

'You mean it was a girlfriend or something?'

'Who knows? A married woman, perhaps, terrified of her husband finding out. Or even a boyfriend. Mrs Provender may not be as broad-minded as you or I.'

Hanbury turned his attention to the other two files. In the second of them he found Miles's passport and a leather-bound address book, which he put to one side without saying anything. The third contained manuals for the various machines which Miles had owned.

'Methodical chap,' Hanbury said, picking up an instruction booklet for a camera. 'Ah. That reminds me.'

'What?'

'Nothing important. We'll discuss it later.'

Hanbury flicked through the booklet. A receipt had been neatly stapled to the cover. He put the booklet with the passport and the address book.

Together they went through the rest of the flat. Miles's toothbrush and his electric razor were in the bathroom, and there was no sign that anyone else was in the habit of using it.

'It might have been as simple as that,' Hanbury murmured to himself. 'Your visitor could have been picking up a toothbrush.'

Dougal uncapped the aftershave and sniffed. 'What do you think?' he said, holding out the bottle.

Hanbury screwed up his face. 'Not what I'd choose myself.'

'Yes but is it the same as the smell in the hall?'

'Almost certainly.'

They went into the bedroom, which contained a double bed, an exercise bicycle and a large fitted wardrobe with mirrored doors. On the walls were pictures of racing cars. Like the rest of the flat, the room was clean, uncluttered and tidy.

'No books,' Dougal said. 'Did you notice?'

'Miles isn't what you'd call a cultured person,' said Hanbury, managing his tenses with his customary aplomb. 'Not in the traditional sense. His interests lie in other fields.'

One side of the wardrobe was entirely empty apart from half a dozen wire hangers and a cricket bat.

Dougal pointed this out to Hanbury. 'Someone did a flit?'

'Who knows?' Hanbury said. 'It may mean something or nothing.' He was investigating the other side of the wardrobe. Without saying anything, he tossed a plump wallet and a cheque-book on to the bed. 'He certainly wasn't after money.'

Dougal worried the point like a sore tooth. 'You agree we can't rule out the possibility of a lover?'

'No indeed.' Hanbury held up an opened packet of condoms. 'Or at least a taste for casual encounters.'

Next, he took out a camera in a case. He opened it. There wasn't a film inside. He put the camera with the other items on the bed.

'No photographs,' Dougal said.

'According to the receipt he only bought the camera a couple of weeks ago.'

'That makes it even stranger.'

'Not necessarily.' Hanbury shut the wardrobe door. 'Perhaps he's just sent off the film to be developed.'

Dougal shrugged.

'That's it, I'm afraid,' Hanbury went on. 'I'll just see if I can find a carrier bag in the kitchen.'

While Hanbury was gone Dougal went into the hall and studied the answering machine. Hanbury returned with his selection of Miles's possessions in another Marks & Spencer carrier bag. He looked first at Dougal, then at the answering machine.

'The answering machine's switched off,' Dougal said. 'And—'

'Good,' Hanbury interrupted. 'I'm glad you've done that. No point in leaving it on.' He opened the front door of the flat and smiled roguishly. 'Now come along. I'm not in the mood for wasting time. I've got a date with a lady.'

They sat in the Jaguar. Hanbury lit a Caporal. Dougal gave him the cheque from Mrs Provender. Hanbury raised his eyebrows.

'You must have impressed her. For that she deserves an interim report. One doesn't want to keep the poor lady in unnecessary suspense. You can use the car phone in a moment.'

'Talking of phones,' Dougal said, 'why hadn't the answering machine got a tape in it?'

Hanbury looked steadily at Dougal. 'How odd,' he said. 'How very odd.'

'Hugo Brassard said he phoned yesterday and got the answering machine. Mrs Provender said the same.'

'The obvious conclusion is that your intruder took the tape.'

'Why?' Dougal asked.

'Because he'd left a message on it, presumably.'

'That means it was someone who knows Miles is missing.'

'Almost certainly it does.' Hanbury smiled. 'You realize that we're talking about a minimum of fifty or sixty people?'

'Nonsense,' Dougal said. 'It must be—'

'Everyone at Brassard Prentisse. All Miles's clients. Mrs Provender. And God knows how many people they've all told. And then there's something you don't know – Miles's secretary came up with his Christmas card list. She'd got it on her word processor. Like so many people these days' – Hanbury allowed himself a disapproving sniff – 'Miles got his secretary to address his personal cards and put them through the office franking machine. Hugo spent most of the afternoon trying to get in touch with everyone on the list. No doubt they've told all *their* friends and relations too. It's tiresome but we have to accept that we're no longer dealing with a closed circle. Miles's disappearance is public property.'

'So what do we do about the tape?'

'You'll report its absence to Mrs Provender.' Hanbury peered into the Marks & Spencer carrier bag. 'You can also say that his wallet, cheque-book and passport are not at the flat. But the most important thing to mention is the tape.'

'I don't follow.'

'Well, it's a good sign, isn't it?' Hanbury smiled brilliantly. 'A little ray of hope, eh? Everyone knows the tape was there yesterday. It's gone today. So what does this suggest to the unbiased investigator such as you or me? Why – that Miles has dropped by and taken it, and perhaps his passport too.

After all, only he and his mother are known to have keys to the flat.'

'You're mad,' Dougal said quietly. 'Or I'm mad.'

'Not at all. It's a matter of how you present it to Mrs Provender. Our extensive checks with the police and hospitals have drawn a blank. None of his friends has heard from him – we still have a few more to contact, but not many. We have found no sign of a struggle or robbery at Miles's flat. We have found no sign of any crime whatsoever. The evidence is admittedly skimpy. But, taken all in all, it suggests that Miles Provender left his flat of his own free will on Sunday or Monday. He returned to his flat briefly, probably today. And he has now disappeared, just as thousands of people do, year in, year out. In time we may trace him, or we may not. It's in the lap of the gods.'

'It's cruel.'

'Because it gives her hope?' Hanbury stubbed out his cigarette impatiently. 'Why's that cruel? I'd say it was quite the reverse. The alternative is to tell her her son is dead. Can you imagine the effect on her? Not to mention the effect on you.'

Dougal said nothing.

'You have to take the consequences, you know,' Hanbury said softly. 'One way or the other. And now we must have a chat about tomorrow.'

'What about it?'

'You're going to Austerford in the morning, remember?' Hanbury rummaged in the Marks & Spencer carrier bag. 'It suddenly occurred to me that I'd forgotten to get you a camera. That's why I borrowed Miles's – in case you have an opportunity to take a snapshot of Georgie for Joan.'

'But what about Miles?'

'What about him? There's not a lot more you can do. We'll keep the routine checks going, of course. And you'd better have a chat with the neighbours, just for the record.'

'Not tonight.'

Hanbury peered at Dougal. 'What you need's a good night's sleep.'

'I've just thought of something else,' Dougal said. 'Celia's keys.'

'Which keys?' Hanbury asked with a touch of irritation.

'The ones she gave Miles so he could get into the Kew house. You took them, didn't you?'

Hanbury nodded. 'I suppose we could leave them in the flat. But on the whole I'm against trying to be too clever.'

'Anyway, people might start asking questions.' And the answers, Dougal thought, wouldn't help Celia cope with Miles's disappearance.

'Just so. I think it would be better if they just disappeared. After all, Miles might have had them in his pocket when he chose to vanish. Out of sight, out of mind, eh? Now where were we? Austerford.'

Hanbury twisted round and picked up a large-format road atlas from the back seat.

'It's very straightforward,' he said, opening the atlas. 'You just run up the A1 as far as Biggleswade.'

Hanbury's finger traced the route. Dougal leaned over to look. His eyes focused on the map. Suddenly his mind made a connection which leapt from the map to the memory of a line of writing seen that morning. Celia's writing. He pulled himself away from Hanbury. He was trembling.

'Then you take the B1040,' Hanbury was saying. 'And when you get to—'

'When you get to Stanford,' Dougal said, his voice rising in pitch and harsh with fear and anger, 'you just follow the signs, don't you? What the hell is going on?'

8

The itching grew worse. Dougal thought that perhaps embarrassment had something to do with it. One tended to sweat when embarrassed and sweating might irritate the bites.

A wave of tiredness rolled over him as he nudged the Sierra into the queue of cars crawling up to the Richmond roundabout. It was the wrong time of day for a traffic jam. The car in front braked suddenly. Dougal stopped only just in time. He knew he shouldn't be driving: he was too tired, too distracted. He noticed that the other cars had their headlights on. He switched on his own.

Somewhere ahead, an invisible blockage must have dissolved. The traffic began to flow smoothly. Driving up Kew Road, with the long wall of Kew Gardens on his left, Dougal remembered how Hanbury had chuckled in a way that implied not amusement but condescension; anger would have been an easier reaction to cope with. He remembered the smell of tobacco and the beige leather upholstery, and the sight of the levers and knobs and dials set in the gleaming walnut veneer on the dashboard; and he remembered himself and Hanbury side by side in the Jaguar parked outside the block of flats where Miles Provender had lived. The memories brought him face to face with a question he couldn't answer: had Hanbury been manipulating him, just as he manipulated the controls of his car?

'There's nothing sinister about it, dear boy. Celia must be doing Georgie's PR. So she went up to Austerford for a meeting this afternoon. Why not?'

Because, Dougal had said, such a gross coincidence was

79

statistically implausible. Because it was easier and safer to believe that it wasn't a coincidence at all.

'Of course it's not a coincidence.' Hanbury had smiled. 'Who said it was?'

'Then what is it?'

'Georgie was merely following up my suggestion.'

Dougal wished his mind would work better. 'Did this come up when you and Georgie met for lunch?'

'Exactly. That's when I heard he was planning to give Joan what he called "the old heave-ho". He had other fish to fry. Those were his exact words.'

Georgie, Hanbury reminded Dougal, had never known the nature of Hanbury's relationship with Joan. The friendship between the two men had continued after Georgie's move to Spain. 'Tepid friendships,' Hanbury remarked, switching briefly into his maxim mode, 'are often curiously enduring.' Every year or so, when Georgie was passing through London, he would phone Hanbury and they would meet for lunch or dinner.

'I told you Georgie hinted he was contemplating some sort of business venture in the UK. A little later on, apropos of nothing in particular, we started talking about public relations. And he asked me what PR company we used, how I rated them. Interesting, don't you think?'

'You mean that if he needed a PR company, he'd got further than merely contemplating?'

Hanbury nodded. 'You don't need a PR company unless you've got something to promote. I said we were fed up with the chaps we were using and that we were planning to try Brassard Prentisse, said they seemed quite competent. But I assumed he hadn't taken me up on it. Naturally I put out a few feelers with Miles – he'd heard nothing. So I thought Georgie must have tried another company.'

Dougal muttered an apology. Making an accusation which turns out to be false is a doubly humiliating process. You have not only wronged the person you accused – you have also demonstrated your own stupidity.

'And now I wonder if you can explain something for me.' Hanbury sounded like a benevolent teacher trying to encourage a backward pupil by asking him one of the few questions he was competent to answer. 'How did you find out that Celia was working for Georgie?'

Dougal told him about the directions he had seen on Celia's pad at the end of their meeting at the BPC office.

'Celia mentioned having a meeting with a client this afternoon,' Hanbury said quickly.

'Hugo Brassard was dying to know what it was all about. Do you remember?'

'Is that possible? They're partners. Wouldn't she have told him?'

Dougal shrugged. 'I know some clients are incredibly paranoid, especially when they're on the verge of a product launch. They don't want to risk a competitor running a spoiling operation.'

Hanbury grunted. 'How very interesting.'

'Why didn't you tell me about recommending Celia?' Dougal asked.

'Two reasons – no, I tell a lie: three reasons. As I say, I thought he hadn't taken me up on the suggestion. Second, and more important, you saw the sort of state Joan was in last night. Tired and emotional, eh? As indeed were you. No point in muddying the waters unnecessarily. You must have noticed how vulnerable Joan is. Particularly where Georgie's concerned.'

Hanbury arranged his features to indicate not only the delicacy of the situation but also his profound concern for Joan. James Hanbury, Dougal thought, friend in need – to Joan as well as to himself; and even, it seemed, a friend of sorts to Georgie Trotwood. He seemed to have forgotten about the third reason, so Dougal reminded him of it.

'Eh? Simply that I haven't had a chance to mention it. By the end of yesterday evening you weren't really in a condition to take in new information. And then today we've been tied up with the absconding Miles. Until now that is. And now I have told you. It's the first chance we've had.'

'Yes,' Dougal said. 'I see.'

'You didn't really think—? Never mind. Why don't you phone Mrs Provender and tell her our good news about Miles? You remember what we – ah – deduced? That he may have been back to the flat since Monday? Qualified good news, yes, and a little hypothetical: but still more good than bad.'

Dougal signalled right and turned into the maze of residential streets to the east of Kew Road. He had made the phone call, conscious all the time of Hanbury beside him; and Mrs Provender had been unbearably grateful for his time and trouble. Then at last Hanbury had let him go for the evening.

The Sierra zigzagged through the side streets. It occurred to Dougal that the business about Hanbury recommending Celia to Georgie had obscured what had happened earlier in Miles's flat: the intruder who had slipped away locking the front door behind him. The intruder might still have been Hanbury. Just because one suspicion centring on Hanbury had proved to be groundless, it didn't follow that other suspicions were groundless too.

Dougal turned into Celia's road and reversed neatly into her drive. Congratulating himself on the unusual tidiness of the manoeuvre, he parked in front of Celia's Volvo. As he turned off the engine, Dougal realized that he was in the wrong place. This was no longer his home. Tiredness and old habits had conspired to make a fool of him.

The lights were on in the sitting room and upstairs. Celia must have heard the sound of his engine. If he drove off at once, she would probably put quite the wrong construction on his action. She might think he had had something to say, a bid for reconciliation perhaps, and that his courage had failed him at the last moment. Or she might worry. Or she'd think him an irritating fool who couldn't stay away.

Dougal scratched a particularly vicious bite just above his left knee. The moment one noticed an itch, a dozen others sprang up and clamoured for attention. He scratched as many as he could reach and got out of the car.

The keys to the house were in his pocket, but using them

might be misconstrued. Dougal rang the front doorbell instead. A moment later Celia answered the door. She was wearing a blue cotton dress he had always liked. Her feet were bare and her hair was tied back. He guessed she had been working. Dougal smiled at her.

'Hello,' she said eagerly. 'Have you got some news?'

He was so tired that the question took him off balance. He blinked foolishly at her. 'News?'

'About Miles.'

'Yes – or rather no. James and I had a look at his flat this evening.'

'And—?'

'Nothing much.' Dismayed by his own stupidity, Dougal heard himself trotting out the lies: 'We couldn't find his wallet, cheque-book or passport. And the tape's gone from the answering machine, which is odd. On the whole it looks as if he left of his own free will.'

She looked grimly at him and said in a neutral voice: 'Is that all?'

Dougal nodded. 'On that subject. I've got a favour to ask.'

'You'd better come in.'

She stood back and he stepped into the hall.

'Maybe I should have phoned.'

'It doesn't matter. What is it?'

'You know that camp bed of your father's? Could I borrow it?'

He had to explain why he needed to borrow it. Mentioning the bedbugs had the undesired effect of arousing her sympathy.

'How awful. Are you sure? Can I see the bites?'

He rolled up his sleeve to show her a few of the angry red marks.

'You can't sleep there,' she said. 'Do you want to come back here until it's sorted out? There's the spare room.'

'No. The camp bed will be fine.' He thought he saw relief in her face.

'They might crawl across the floor in search of you.'

'Like heat-seeking missiles? I don't think they're long-range animals. I'll get it, shall I?'

When she nodded he went upstairs. He found the camp bed. Celia came out of the sitting room as he was carrying it down the stairs.

'Have you eaten?' she said. 'I was just about to have something.'

To his surprise, Dougal discovered that he was enormously hungry. The pizza he had eaten before going to Miles's flat was no more than an unpleasant memory. He followed Celia into the kitchen. They loaded a tray with cheese, fruit and biscuits. Celia produced an opened bottle of Macon Villages from the fridge. Dougal fetched the glasses.

They took the tray into the sitting room. It looked as if Celia had emptied her briefcase on to the sofa. She scooped up papers, files, discs, notebooks and pens and dumped them on to an armchair. Dougal put down the tray on the octagonal table between the sofa and the chair. The table belonged to him. He glanced at Celia, who was moving towards the door, and decided not to jog her memory. His eyes slipped down to the papers on the armchair. Automatically he read the heading on the blue envelope file on top of the heap. It said: AUSTERFORD 2000.

'I forgot the olives,' Celia said.

She went to fetch them from the kitchen. Dougal felt breathless. He stared at the file and fought the temptation to lift the flap. Prying in this house seemed a particularly sordid thing to do. On the other hand, a glimpse of the contents could be so useful. It might even obviate the need to go to Austerford in the morning and face unknown problems. In the long run, it might even help Celia.

'I brought some rolls too,' Celia said behind him. 'Have you tried them? They're from Marks and Sparks.'

Dougal thought of the bag over Miles's head.

'I think I'll have a biscuit, thanks. Shall I pour the wine?'

They sat at opposite ends of the long sofa. Dougal ate a few mouthfuls, drank half a glass of wine, and discovered that his appetite had mysteriously disappeared.

'I nearly forgot,' Celia said. 'I meant to ask you about the keys.'

'Of course. You'll want them back.'

Dougal put down the glass and felt in his trouser pocket for his set of keys for the house. He caught sight of the file again. Perhaps Celia would leave the room to make coffee or go to the lavatory.

'No – keep them,' she said.

Surprised, he looked at her. She was concentrating on cutting herself a wedge of Vignotte.

'You may need them.' She paused, then added hurriedly: 'If you're bringing Eleanor home and I'm not in. Just in case.'

'OK.'

'By the way, have you got two sets?'

'No.' He wondered if in his new role as a guest he could actually ask for coffee. It wouldn't take long just to get an idea of the file's contents. The very thought made him feel excited and simultaneously disgusted. Usually such a tactic wouldn't have had this effect. He had long since learned to live with the fact that his job was an ethical quagmire; work was something that part of him did while the other part watched, detached, sardonic and reserving judgement. But this convenient arrangement failed to work now Celia was involved.

'It doesn't matter,' Celia was saying. 'The way things are going I shan't need them much longer.'

'What?'

'You remember what I told you this morning?'

'About the Provenders?'

She nodded. Mrs Provender was considering investing in Brassard Prentisse Communications, in which case Miles would have become a full partner. In effect she would have given the money to Miles and he would have used it to buy into the company.

Celia picked up the bottle. 'I – I wasn't entirely honest. The money wouldn't just be convenient. It's vital.'

Dougal held out his glass. He remembered the untenanted desks and the shrouded word processors.

'Do you mean the company's at risk?'

'We've lost a lot of clients – not our fault; because of the recession. Clients who owe us money have gone bankrupt. And Hugo and I were stupid. We thought we'd just keep growing.'

'A lot of people made the same mistake.'

She ignored him. 'We let the overheads get too high. We're lumbered with a lease we can't afford. It was overexpensive to begin with, and we had to borrow from the bank. Now there's just not enough money coming in to cope with our commitments. The bank and the property company are acting like *shits*. And our accountants and even our lawyer aren't much better. They're afraid they won't get paid.'

She noticed the bottle in her hand. She topped up his glass. It was very unlike her to describe anyone as a *shit*.

'Could you extend the mortgage on the house?'

'I did that months ago. Hugo's done the same.'

She looked away to refill her own glass. She was near tears, Dougal thought, but she wasn't going to give in. It looked as if he had killed Celia's company as well as her lover. At last he understood about the keys.

'You're going to sell the house,' he said, making it a statement.

'No choice. Not that I'll get what I paid. But I can't afford the mortgage.' She stared angrily at him. 'I'm not asking for help. Even for Eleanor's sake.'

'I know. I'm not offering it.'

'Anyway, you couldn't help. You earn too little.' She glanced at him. 'Sorry. I shouldn't have said that.'

'It's true.' Dougal was used to her low opinion of his earning ability. 'What happens if the Provenders invest?'

'Then at least there's hope. Otherwise the company will fold.'

'Wouldn't the money just put off the evil day?'

'I don't think so. Things are just beginning to look up. If we hold on to the Custodemus account, that'll help. And I've got another new account in the pipeline.' Her eyes drifted towards the folder. 'It might generate quite a lot of money. But it'll take time.'

'What's that?' Dougal said; he tried desperately hard to speak casually – the result sounded as though he were stifling a yawn.

'Potentially it's very big but it's still at the development stage. I had to sign one of those letters of confidentiality. Even Hugo doesn't know the details yet. The client's so security-conscious I had to promise to work on it away from the office.'

'Is that normal?'

'These days the client makes all the rules.' She hesitated, and Dougal guessed she was working out how much she could legitimately tell him. 'Admittedly, this one's a bit odd. But he seems on the level and I can't afford to pick and choose.'

Celia ate a few more mouthfuls and then put down her plate. She nursed her glass and stared at the empty fireplace. Meanwhile Dougal peeled an apple and tried not to allow her remark about his income to rankle. He worked part time for Custodemus, which was quite enough for sanity. Perhaps he should ask Hanbury for a rise. He watched Celia's profile and read despair in her face; and he wondered whether it was due to the imminent collapse of her company or Miles's disappearance. Either way he was to blame.

Suddenly she looked at him and said, as if she'd been listening to his thoughts: 'I can't understand what Miles is up to. It's so unlike him. Unless he's had an accident or something.'

Dougal shrugged. For a while Celia said nothing, and he thought the silence would never end.

'I thought I was so bloody clever.' She waved a hand in a gesture that included the house, the car, the business and perhaps Miles as well. 'All this – I'd done it all by myself.'

'So you did. That hasn't changed.'

'But it hasn't lasted. So was it worth it in the first place? Maybe I should have stayed at home with Eleanor. Maybe I should—' She stopped abruptly, and looked at him with hot, angry eyes. 'Can you imagine what it'd be like, having to start again? I don't think I could bear it.'

9

As Dougal was going into Austerford post office, he almost
collided with a small Japanese man in a pinstripe suit and gold-
framed glasses. The Japanese was carrying a picture postcard.

Dougal smiled apologetically, and so did the Japanese. The
Japanese took a pace backwards, yielding the right of way, and
so did Dougal. Dougal took a step to his right, and the Japanese
executed a mirror-image movement to his left.

'Please,' Dougal said desperately. 'I insist.'

The Japanese grinned and Dougal grinned back. The
tendency of two strangers to converge on a collision course is
one of those mysterious behavioural phenomena which appear
to have no biological basis and yet transcend cultural differences.

Dougal stepped backwards again. The Japanese came out of
the shop. He was immediately followed by another Japanese
with a postcard – this one almost identical to the first man
except that he wasn't wearing glasses. Then came a third in a
grey suit; he was carrying a briefcase as well as a postcard.

A large Toyota saloon was waiting at the kerb. Dougal had
already noticed it because it was painted white and so brilliantly
polished that it hurt the eyes. A uniformed chauffeur with
European features got out and opened the nearside doors. The
three Japanese men got into the car. As the car drove away,
one of the rear windows slid down, and the first Japanese
nodded goodbye.

Dougal looked after the Toyota. The moment of shared
amusement had cheered him up. Things were improving. No
doubt this was partly because he had slept for eight uninter-
rupted hours on Celia's camp bed; he did not remember his

dreams. And now it was Wednesday, over two and a half days since Miles's death. Time the healer, Dougal thought, or rather time the smoother-over of uncomfortable memories.

He went into the shop. A spring-mounted bell tinkled above his head. The interior was cool and dark – a relief after the glare of the sun. His eyes took a moment to adjust.

A woman was saying, 'It stands to reason, doesn't it? Corsets aren't what they used to be.'

'The bottom's fallen out of the market.' A man cackled. 'That's what I say.'

'Maybe,' remarked another woman. 'But she's not short of a bob or two. And I'd better pay for the papers while I'm here.'

A counter ran continuously along the sides and back of the shop. On the left, sheltered by a grill, was the post-office part of the establishment. In the rest of the space, the proprietors had made a brave attempt to stock everything else the customer might need.

'It's all him,' said the first woman in a querulous voice like a rusty hinge. 'He's got her wrapped round his little finger.'

An old man shuffled through a bead curtain over a doorway at the back of the shop. 'Little finger?' he said with another cackle. 'It's not his finger that does it.'

The first woman hushed him. 'Why don't you make yourself useful? Serve the gentleman.'

'I'd like a couple of films, please,' Dougal said. 'And a postcard.'

He caught sight of the films he wanted on one of the shelves behind the counter, and pointed them out to the old man.

There seemed to be only one postcard available. Dougal examined it while the man wrestled with the electronic till. The picture showed Austerford church, a brick building which looked as though it had been designed as a neo-Gothic engine shed for a turn-of-the-century railway station. Dougal thought it was an unlovely object, but perhaps the three Japanese had perceived beauties invisible to occidental eyes. Meanwhile he listened to the two women arguing about the amount of the newspaper bill.

The old man dropped Dougal's change on the counter. Most

of it rolled on to the floor, some behind the counter, some in front. Everyone joined in the search for the coins. This shared pursuit, which eventually reached a successful conclusion, put all four of them in a good temper.

'By the way,' Dougal said as he was leaving, 'can you tell me where to find Yew Tree Cottage? I'm looking for Mr Vane.'

There was a sudden silence.

'There's a lane goes off beyond the church,' the first woman said curtly. 'Down there on the right.'

'Is it far? Do I need to drive?' It might be better if Vane didn't see Dougal's car.

'Not unless you've lost the use of your legs,' the old man said.

Dougal went outside. The merciless heat enveloped him. The sun was directly overhead. It blazed from a harsh blue sky without a cloud in sight. On the other side of the road was the village green, an irregular quadrilateral of grass. The village was smaller than he had expected. It consisted chiefly of semi-detached agricultural cottages which shared a strong family resemblance with the church, punctuated here and there with houses and bungalows built in the last twenty years. The church was about fifty yards away on the same side of the green as the post office.

The Ford Sierra was parked a short distance away on the other side of the road. Dougal sat in the driving seat and put a film in Miles's camera with the help of the manual. The camera looked virtually idiot-proof, which was just as well. He decided to take it with him to Yew Tree Cottage together with the manual and the spare film in case he proved to be even more idiotic than the camera's Japanese designers had anticipated. It was too hot to wear a jacket so he locked it in the boot of the car along with his wallet.

Apart from the camera, which he carried in its case slung over his shoulder, the only thing he took with him was two hundred and fifty pounds in cash. Hanbury had produced the money yesterday evening after their visit to Miles's flat – 'This should cover your immediate running expenses. Don't worry about receipts. Let me know if you need more.' Using cash was sensible because it was untraceable. Nevertheless Hanbury's willingness to dig into his pocket had made Dougal instantly wary. Hanbury believed in getting value for money, particularly when it was his own money rather than the company's.

Dougal walked slowly through the heat to the church. A couple of cars passed him but he saw no one on foot. The mouth of the lane was on the far side of the church. He cut across the churchyard and came out on to the lane at a point opposite a driveway barred by a pair of gates. The gates were closed. On either side of them was a tall brick wall with the branches of trees visible behind it. There was a lodge cottage set back from the road beside the drive. Beside it were two notices. One said: NO PUBLIC RIGHT OF WAY. TRESPASSERS WILL BE PROSECUTED. The second depicted the head of a slavering dog, below which were the words: GO ON. BREAK IN. MAKE HIS DAY.

Yew Tree Cottage was a few yards further on the same side of the lane as the church. Its garden actually bordered on the churchyard. There was a clump of yews beside the church and one of them had strayed into the garden. The cottage's flower-beds were full of weeds and the grass was knee-high. Near the yew stood a rusting swing. A washing line laden with men's clothes ran between them. The clothes were wrinkled and varying shades of grey.

Dougal opened the gate – modern, made of wrought iron and set in an asymmetrical arch built of reconstituted stone. Instantly dogs began to bark. Two Alsatians appeared round the side of the house. They hurtled down the cracked concrete path towards Dougal.

He jumped back into the lane and slammed the gate. The animals did not give up. One tried to leap over the gate while the other tried to burrow under it. All the while they snapped and barked. The gate rattled and creaked. Their impotence increased their fury. Dougal tried to remember if there was a telephone box on the green.

There was a shout like a snarl: 'Shut up, you buggers.'

A thickset man limped down the path from the side of the house. He had a black beard and kept his face screwed up as though he were staring at the sun. His body was out of proportion. The top half looked lean and muscular, but the bottom half was thick and flabby. The general impression was of a body running to seed from the bottom up. His limp made him look like a sailor crossing the deck of a ship in a storm. He was carrying two leather leads.

The dogs took no notice of him. They continued to do their best to tear Dougal from limb to limb.

'Mr Vane?' Dougal called above the racket.

The man paid no attention. He reached the dogs and slashed their flanks repeatedly with the leads. 'Get off with you!' he yelled. 'Or I'll bloody kill you!'

At first the dogs ignored him. Their master tried to kick them – a difficult manoeuvre for him to accomplish because he was so unsteady on his legs. Yelping with excitement himself, he flogged them even harder. Eventually the dogs realized what was happening. They slunk away.

'Bloody animals,' Vane said. He was breathing heavily and looked pleased with himself.

'I'm Nicholas Marston,' Dougal said. 'I phoned you earlier this morning.'

Vane unlatched the gate. 'Come inside.'

Seen at close quarters, his complexion was an ominous chalky colour. His skin was pocked with craters. There was a colony of blackheads on his large, fleshy nose. He wore sagging jeans and a faded blue shirt with a frayed collar.

He rolled up the path with Dougal beside him. 'How d'you get my name?'

'Yellow Pages,' Dougal said.

Vane grunted. 'You're the first client who's said that. Cost the earth, that advert.'

He opened the front door and ushered Dougal through an untidy hall into a little sitting room dominated by an enormous television. The ceiling was covered with textured paint and plywood beams arranged in a criss-cross pattern like the bars of a cage. One wall had been stripped back to the brick. The television had pride of place within an inglenook fireplace built of the reconstituted stone used for the archway in the garden. There was a pair of dirty socks in the middle of the carpet and a pile of empty crisp packets in one of the grey plastic armchairs. The dogs were whining on the other side of the open window.

'They're getting up a petition about the dogs,' Vane said. 'Bastards.'

'Who are?'

'People in the village. I need those dogs. Protection, see? But they call them a public nuisance. It's not really the dogs they object to, it's me.' His voice lurched upwards in pitch and acquired a mincing gentility. 'They think a private detective lowers the tone of the place.'

'I'd have said you're an amenity.'

Vane shrugged. 'There are complications.' He sat down on the arm of one of the chairs and waved Dougal to another. 'What can I do for you then? Background information you said? What on?'

'The people at the Hall.'

'Eh?'

'Mr and Mrs Sutcombe, isn't it?'

Vane screwed up his face even more tightly than before. He looked as if he was trying to cry. 'Why d'you want to know?'

'I'm a journalist. I'm trying to put together a series of articles on people who can afford to live in big houses. It's amazing how many still do. And not just the very rich. The public enjoys finding out how they make ends meet.'

'Why don't you ask them yourself?'

'I will. But I'd like to get some background first. Features like this need more than one viewpoint. I won't quote you by name, of course, not if you don't want me to.'

'Sorry.' Vane struggled to his feet. 'I've got a living to earn.'

'I know that. I'll pay. I don't want gossip, you see. I want an informed professional view.'

'Minimum consultation fee's twenty-five quid. That buys you twenty minutes.'

Dougal peeled off two notes from the wad in his pocket and held them out. Vane took them, examined them quickly and put them in his pocket.

'I'll get you a receipt.' He swayed across the room to the door, where he glanced back. 'Want a coffee or something? I'm going to have some.'

'No thanks.'

'Won't be a moment.'

Vane left the room, shutting the door behind him. The money seemed to have made him almost amiable. Dougal listened to the whining of the dogs and examined the decor. It was almost as hot in the house as it was outside. Time passed slowly and unpleasantly. Vane was gone for less than five minutes but it seemed much more.

He came back with a mug of coffee and a scribbled receipt. Dougal smelled the sweat on him and saw the moisture streaming down his face and damp patches under his arms.

'The Sutcombes,' Dougal prompted. According to the briefing Hanbury had given him last night, the phone at Austerford Hall was registered in the name of Mrs Kathy Sutcombe. Two months earlier it had been in the name of Mrs Kathy Davies.

Vane perched on the arm of the chair again. 'George and Katherine. Georgie and Kathy to their friends. The house belongs to her. Inherited it from her first husband. He owned a corset factory in Bedford.'

'Declining market?'

Vane shrugged. 'It's still going. But yes, I don't think they're making the profits they used to when old Davies was alive. He was the first husband. Family firm. The Sutcombes don't manage the factory themselves. The old man used to, and maybe that's why he made more money.'

Dougal remembered the ostensible purpose of his visit. 'How long have they owned the Hall?'

'Davies bought it after the war. It's a great big barracks of a place. I wouldn't live there if you paid me.'

'So he wasn't born to it?'

'Nor was she. Her dad used to run the pub on the green.'

'What sort of a man's the second husband?'

'Why aren't you taking notes?' Vane said sharply. 'That's a camera, isn't it, not a tape recorder.'

'I've got an aural version of a photographic memory,' Dougal said modestly, wishing he'd had the sense to bring such an obvious prop with him. 'Not a hundred per cent perfect but it's pretty good. You were telling me about Mr Sutcombe.'

The doorbell chimed.

'Won't be a moment.'

Vane shuffled to the door. Dougal thought: but the dogs didn't bark. He stood up and went to the open window. This overlooked the path at the side of the house. The dogs were no longer outside. He couldn't see the gate.

Vane appeared at the corner of the house – so suddenly that Dougal didn't have time to withdraw into the room. The dogs pattered at his heels; they eyed Dougal with malevolent interest. Vane stopped, a dog on each side of him and their leads dangling from his right hand. He looked surprised to see Dougal at the window and unexpectedly shamefaced. And he also looked like a guard detailed to block a possible escape route. The dogs surged forward and snarled softly.

'What is it?' Dougal said.

'Sorry about this.'

'About what?'

Dougal knew the answer even before he heard the footstep behind him. He whirled round. For an instant there seemed to be all the time in the world, in fact far too much of it: time to remember the treacherous release he felt when the hammer tapped Miles's skull; time to remember Celia and Mr and Mrs Provender; time to remember Hanbury's confident and subtly patronizing explanation of why there were absolutely no risks about this little job; time to regret his own failure to run a preliminary check on Vane; and most of all time to feel trapped.

In the doorway of the sitting room was a thin, stooping man whose head almost touched the lintel. He wore dark glasses which completely masked his eyes. He was dressed in brightly coloured shorts, a T-shirt and trainers. His right hand was deep in the pocket of the shorts. He had brown, curly hair and he was beginning to go bald at the front.

'That's his camera case on the chair,' Vane said through the window. 'And I gave him a receipt. I'd better have it back.'

The man nodded. He waved imperiously at Dougal. His skin had a fading but evenly distributed tan.

'Why?' Dougal said. 'I don't understand.'

'If I were you,' Vane said, 'I'd do what he wants. For your own good, I mean.'

The thin man took his hand out of his pocket. He was holding a Stanley knife with great care because the blade was already out. Without warning he slashed the tip along the top of one of the armchairs. Two parallel lines a fraction of an inch apart appeared in the grey plastic.

'Two blades separated by a coin,' Vane explained; he seemed to take the damage to his furniture in his stride. 'Very nasty. It means the cuts are just about impossible to suture. So do as he wants, Mr Marston. That's my advice to you. All right?'

Dougal took the receipt out of his pocket. He let it flutter to the floor.

'You'll be hearing from my solicitor,' he said to Vane. His voice shook a little.

'I doubt that.'

The thin man seemed to lose patience. He advanced from the doorway, grabbed Dougal's arm above the elbow and squeezed until Dougal cried out with pain. He pulled Dougal towards the door. At first Dougal tried to free himself, but the man overcame his resistance with a one-handed casualness that smacked of contempt. The other hand, which was holding the Stanley knife in reserve, scooped up the camera case from the chair.

In the cluttered hallway, Dougal looked up at the blank, tanned face. 'Mr Sutcombe? Is this how you usually treat visitors?'

The man ignored him. He towed Dougal out of the front door and on to the path. The gate was open. Vane was standing in the lane beyond with the dogs on their leads.

'All clear,' he called.

The thin man led Dougal down the path. Everyone looked up and down the lane. No one else was in sight. One of the gates near the lodge was open. Dougal, flanked by Vane and the dogs on one side and the thin man on the other, was led across the roadway and into the drive. They waited for a moment to allow Vane to close the gate behind them.

'It's just one of those things, Mr Marston,' Vane said to Dougal. 'Nothing personal.'

'"Ex-Detective Sergeant, CID,"' Dougal said, quoting Vane's advertisement in the Yellow Pages. '"Confidentiality Assured." What did they kick you out of the police for?'

'Shut up,' Vane said.

The long drive wound into the distance. Once there had been an evenly spaced row of copper beeches on either side, but many of these were no more than stumps. There was no sign of a house, but almost certainly the drive led to Austerford Hall. Cattle were grazing in the nearest open part of the park. The lodge backed on to a thick and untidy belt of woodland. There were several slates missing from the roof of the cottage and one of its pointed windows was broken. But there was a rusting Austin Princess parked outside, and someone had been making a determined effort to clear the garden. As they drew nearer Dougal heard rock music playing inside.

Vane and the dogs left them at the lodge. The thin man pulled Dougal away from the drive and into a track which led round the back of the lodge and into the wood. Dougal stumbled over deep tyre ruts in the dried mud.

'I think there must be some sort of misunderstanding, Mr Sutcombe. Couldn't we discuss it?'

The man might have been deaf for all the notice he took.

He urged Dougal on. The wood closed in around them. The track began to zigzag down a gentle slope. Dougal lost all sense of direction. The man was walking at such a pace that Dougal almost had to run to keep up. He was very thirsty. He made another attempt to start up a conversation but with no better result than he had had before. He waited for an opportunity to try to escape. None came. Even if he succeeded in breaking the man's grip, there would still be the long legs and the Stanley knife to reckon with.

The track made a ninety-degree turn to the left. Set on the slope below them, a few yards away from the track, was a small brick building like a squat tower. There were no visible windows. The only opening was a door.

Still holding on to Dougal, his captor fished out a bunch of keys, selected one and opened the door. He pushed Dougal inside with enough force to send him sprawling on the stone-flagged floor. He lobbed the camera case into a corner and slammed the door. Dougal raised his head and listened. He heard the key turning in the lock.

Dougal stood up. He was shivering – partly from fear and partly because it was surprisingly cool. He was in a high, square chamber with unplastered brick walls and a timber ceiling that had once been painted white or cream. The room was empty, and the lack of dust on the floor suggested that it had been recently swept.

He rattled the handle on the door, which was constructed of thick planks of a heavy wood like oak. He would have needed a sledgehammer to make much impression on it.

Opposite the door was a barred window whose sill was level with Dougal's head. The window was about twice as wide as it was high. The frame was divided into four horizontal rows of ten lights. Each light was about the size of a page from a large book. The glass and the glazing bars were grey with grime and cobwebs. One of the lights – three across, two down – was broken. The sill was at least eighteen inches deep.

Dougal scrambled up to it. He grazed his elbow. The sill

was even filthier than the glass. Long ago a bird had nested here, and there were ample mementoes of its tenancy. Dougal wriggled into a crouching position and raised his face to the broken light. It looked as if someone had thrown a stone or a ball through it many years before. Triangular fragments of glass still clung to the glazing bars.

Beyond it was the brilliant green of grassland in the sun. Dougal's prison was at the apex of a small triangular meadow; there were spurs of woodland on either side and at the bottom a fence made of iron railings. Beyond the fence was another, much larger meadow, which swept gently downhill to a ha-ha about a hundred yards away; the ha-ha protected a lawn leading up to what could only be the garden front of Austerford Hall. If the church and the cottages in the village looked as if they had strayed from a railway station of the last century, here was the terminus itself – enormous, built of red brick, and Gothic in inspiration if not in actuality. A row of Early English french windows opened on to a terrace resembling a miniature viaduct.

Dougal's attention locked on to the one moving figure in this picture. Sutcombe was loping across the second meadow towards the ha-ha. Presumably he was heading for the house. What or who did he want? Why hadn't he questioned Dougal, or even searched him? Because something more important demanded his attention? Above all, why had Sutcombe reacted so violently to the news that a journalist was questioning one of his neighbours about him? If he wanted to stall Dougal, surely there were other, less foolhardy methods which would have been just as effective and much less dangerous?

There weren't any answers. Either Sutcombe was a fool, which seemed unlikely, or his actions were partly dictated by considerations that Dougal knew nothing about. In the meantime, Dougal thought, the best thing he could do was keep busy and keep his options open.

He dangled his legs over the sill, turned on to his stomach and slithered back to the floor. He picked up the camera case, which was made of grey nylon and heavily padded. Inside were

99

two compartments – one containing the spare film and the manual, the other the camera itself.

The camera looked all right despite the treatment it had received. Dougal pointed it at the window and pressed the shutter. The flash worked; so did the motor driving the film. He took out the empty film canister and put it beside the case on the floor. He then took out the new film and removed its packaging so that it was ready to load.

Leaving the case on the floor, Dougal put the camera on the sill and climbed back beside it. He peered through the broken window. There was no one to be seen. He used the built-in telephoto lens to take a photograph of the house. Then he waited.

With increasing desperation he tried to distract his mind from a succession of nightmare scenarios. He also grew colder and colder, which seemed a bizarre fate on such a warm day. He wondered if there really were dogs on the loose in the park. Surely not during the day? Maybe Vane rented his rabid monsters to the Sutcombes at night-time.

The longer Dougal waited, the worse it was. Inaction left him with no defence against fear. Nor was his body in training for perching indefinitely on a window-sill: soon his muscles were protesting.

He tried to plan what he would do when Sutcombe returned. He might stand a chance of escaping if he could get among the trees, which looked as if they hadn't been coppiced for decades, and somehow work his way back to the car. The village green couldn't be more than half a mile away, though Dougal wasn't sure in which direction. But if escape failed or if he lacked the courage even to try, as seemed all too probable, he would have to try negotiation.

The journalistic cover had not been designed to stand up to questioning; he had an out-of-date NUJ card in the name of 'Nicholas Marston' in the car, but all his other documentation was in his real name. It was too late to construct a more convincing set of lies. There was no point in preserving a heroic silence because if Sutcombe was as ruthless as they said he was, he wouldn't object to using a little torture. If necessary, Dougal decided, he would tell the truth. It offered him the best chance of surviving relatively undamaged. Sutcombe would surely calculate that Dougal would be more of a help than a hindrance if alive and co-operative.

Dougal told himself that the question of loyalty didn't enter into it. His physical safety was at stake. Besides this wasn't his quarrel. He didn't want to be involved. This was between Sutcombe, Joan and Hanbury. He also knew that he could not rely on Hanbury to come riding to the rescue. Hanbury was not a knight errant, and he tended to conduct his personal relationships on a profit-and-loss basis.

At last he saw movement on the lawn in front of the house. Two men were walking from one end of the terrace towards a flight of steps leading down the ha-ha to a gate. One was Sutcombe – still in his shorts and T-shirt. The other was a man of roughly the same size and build, but dressed in a blazer and cream trousers. They came through the gate and set out across the meadow towards Dougal's prison.

Using the telephoto lens, Dougal started shooting as soon as there was a chance that the faces were near enough to produce a recognizable photograph. He had shot all the film by the time they were twenty yards from the building he was in. The film whirred as it rewound itself automatically. The two men veered to their left, presumably to bring them round to the door of the room containing their prisoner.

Dougal rolled from the sill. He landed on the floor with a thud that jarred his bones. He snapped open the back of the camera and ripped out the film. He put it in its plastic canister, clipped on the lid and stuffed the canister down the front of his pants. With shaking hands he put the new film inside the camera. The motor whirred again as it wound the film up to the first frame. While it was still moving, Dougal crammed the camera and the packaging for the new film into the case. He fastened the catch.

A key scraped in the lock.

Dougal bounded backwards, leaving the case on the ground. He leaned against the wall and tried to quieten his breathing. His hands and clothes were filthy. He found this obscurely disquieting.

The door opened with a rush, as if pushed. The first inside, wary like a dog in a strange house, was the man in shorts; he had his Stanley knife in his hand. He glanced at Dougal and then from side to side. Satisfied that Dougal had arranged no surprises, he stood by the door. The man in the blazer followed him in. He nodded to the first man, who shut the door and stood in front of it. Dougal realized that he had made a mistake.

'Mr Sutcombe?' he said to the man in the blazer. 'Mr George Sutcombe?'

'Why are you asking?'

'I'm a journalist,' Dougal said. 'Nicholas Marston. How do you do?'

'Pleased to meet you,' Georgie said. 'I hope my employee hasn't – well, given you the wrong idea, if you know what I mean?'

Dougal's hopes rose. 'I can't understand what he and Vane are up to. They kidnapped me. Your employee threatened me with a knife.'

Georgie glanced at the man in shorts. 'You crapbrain.' He turned back to Dougal. 'We've had a bit of trouble in the past. We have to be careful. Still there's no excuse for him over-reacting like that.'

'But Georgie—'

Franky-Boy? Dougal remembered Joan's words: *He's like Georgie's dog. He's not right in the head. There's something missing.* And he remembered how she'd begun to tremble.

A muscle in Franky-Boy's face was twitching. 'But I had to do something,' he pleaded in an unexpectedly high-pitched voice. 'I tried to find you when Vane rang.'

'But you couldn't. So you used your bloody initiative, eh?' Georgie looked at Dougal again. His face was still hard and suspicious. 'And for all we know that's just as well. What exactly are you doing here?'

It was neatly done, Dougal thought: Georgie was keeping

both of them on edge. On the principle that there was no point in giving away information unnecessarily, Dougal trotted out the story he had given Vane, and very thin it sounded. He clamped his arms across his chest in the hope that it would make the fact he was trembling less obvious. While he talked he examined his captors.

The two men were completely different but you could have described them with many of the same words. Both were tall, thin and slightly stooping; both were wiry and tanned; both had clean-shaven, bony faces and receding hairlines; both were well into middle age.

Franky-Boy's eyes wandered anxiously between Dougal and his master. It was possible that the strong, silent exterior concealed nothing more frightening than emotional insecurity and stupidity, though that was bad enough when allied to physical strength and a habit of obedience to someone like Georgie Sutcombe, formerly Trotwood. It wasn't difficult to imagine him throwing Joan from a balcony.

Georgie, dapper in cravat and double-breasted blazer, went through the camera case while Dougal talked. He found the catch on the back of the camera, opened it and took out the unexposed film. He checked the case and found the packaging for it. He glanced at the manual.

'I know we all make mistakes,' Dougal said, galloping towards his conclusion. 'Security must be a major problem with a place like this. Your employee just got a little over-enthusiastic. So if you let me go immediately, I'll say no more about it.'

Georgie looked up. 'Lean against the wall with your hands over your head,' he said.

'I don't understand.'

'You don't have to understand, Mr Marston. Just do it.'

'But why?'

'Because your name isn't Marston, is it?' Georgie glanced at the manual in his hand – no, Dougal realized with a jolt of horror, not at the manual: at the credit card receipt stapled to its cover. 'It's Miles J. Provender.'

IO

But Miles was miles away.

'He's a friend of mine,' Dougal said. 'He lent me his camera. I'm Nick Marston.'

'Oh yeah,' Georgie said. 'And I'm the Archbishop of Canterbury.'

He nodded to Franky-Boy. Franky-Boy put one hand on Dougal's collar and the other, which was still holding the Stanley knife, on Dougal's shoulder. Dougal spun through a hundred and eighty degrees and found himself facing the bare bricks.

'If you don't put your hands up, Miles,' Georgie said, 'he'll rub your snout in that wall.'

Dougal did as he was told. His forearms were speckled with goose pimples. There were footsteps behind him.

'Don't move an inch,' Georgie whispered, and his breath tickled Dougal's left ear. 'Not an *inch*.'

Something cool touched Dougal's neck.

'It's my friend's knife,' Georgie said. 'It's resting on the artery.'

A hand felt its way into the left-hand pocket of the failed rubber-planter's trousers. The fingers closed round the key on its tag.

'So you got a car – eh, Miles? A Ford. Where is it?'

'In the village,' Dougal said. 'And I'm not Miles.'

'Where in the village?'

'Near the post office.'

'We'll have to do something about that.' Georgie let go of the key. His other hand tried the right-hand pocket, which was empty. He moved to the back pocket of Dougal's trousers and unbuttoned the flap. 'What have we here? Loose change, eh?

Over two hundred pounds. You *have* come well provided. You were generous with Vane too.' Georgie pushed the roll of notes back into Dougal's pocket. 'You must have a wallet and so on. Where?'

'In the boot of the car,' Dougal said.

'You can put your hands down. We're going to relocate you. Find you somewhere cooler.'

Dougal lowered his arms and slowly turned round. Georgie and Franky-Boy were by the door.

'Look, Mr Sutcombe, if you want to know the truth—'

'The truth?' Georgie interrupted. 'Of course I want the truth. But I want to be sure it *is* the truth. You've told me one pack of lies already. There's only one way to be absolutely one hundred per cent sure that you're not going to tell me another. Can you guess what it is, Miles?'

Franky-Boy made an involuntary noise, a giggle cut short in the middle. Dougal glanced at him. His eyes were moist, and he was chewing his lips. He looked like a schoolboy examining the centrefold of a pornographic magazine.

'On second thoughts,' Georgie went on, 'don't even try to guess. We'll give you a full demonstration when we come back.'

Osmond Mac, when are you coming back? Ooh – ooh . . .

'Osmond Mac,' Dougal said on impulse, knowing there was nothing to lose. 'What about that?'

Georgie's face sharpened, as though the individual features had suddenly become more prominent. He leapt forward and grabbed Dougal's shoulders. His long thin lips were squeezed together. He stared at Dougal with blank eyes. His hands moved together and tightened round Dougal's neck. Dougal tensed himself to struggle.

'Ah,' Georgie said, and the hands relaxed. 'So that's it. Nice to know where we are.'

Releasing Dougal, he glanced at Franky-Boy and pointed to the floor. Franky-Boy nodded. Georgie picked up the camera case, opened the door and went outside. Franky-Boy gripped Dougal's right arm. Please God, Dougal prayed with the shameless fervency of the temporary believer, I need a miracle. As they left the room the warm air enveloped him, and he realized how cold he had become.

They followed Georgie round the corner of the building. A path of dried mud descended in steep and irregular steps next to the side wall, which had neither door nor window. Franky-Boy kept Dougal between him and the wall. The undergrowth, a tangle of brambles, gorse and saplings, pressed close to the building; it looked impassable, even if Dougal succeeded in escaping from his guard.

Dougal caught sight of the meadows and the Hall beyond. Georgie rounded the corner. Franky-Boy tugged Dougal's arm, urging him on. They stumbled into the sunlight. And simultaneously Dougal stumbled into the miracle.

'Cooee!' a woman's voice called. 'Georgie! It's me!'

'Oh Christ,' Franky-Boy muttered.

For a moment he hesitated as if wondering whether to retreat. Dougal pulled them both forward. In a couple of seconds he assimilated a vast quantity of information. The woman was only a few yards away; she was approaching from the direction of the fence. She had seen all three of them already. Georgie almost leapt towards her. Franky-Boy let go of Dougal's arm.

The newcomer was large, dark and dumpy. Dougal guessed she was about forty – roughly the same age as Joan Trotwood, though there was no other similarity between them apart from their shared gender. Her face had a low forehead, heavy brows and a projecting jaw; but her smile as she looked up at Georgie made it almost beautiful. She was wearing a long brown pinafore dress resembling a badly made sack.

'I thought I saw you and Frank coming over here. You haven't forgotten it's nearly lunchtime?'

On Dougal's left the front of the tower loomed above him. The building's character seemed to have changed, as if by magic. It had become a miniature stately home entirely faced with stone. The slope of the ground made the front elevation much taller than the rear. At either corner a stone staircase swept up to a grand front door with tall windows on either side. A balustrade ran along the top of the building. Urns stood on the corners. Underneath the front door, recessed beneath the double flight of steps, was the window of the room where Dougal had been held. Several yards beneath the window was another, more plebeian flight of steps which descended to a heavy wooden door below ground level. On either side of these steps were stone benches.

'Darling, you shouldn't have walked all this way in the heat.' Georgie took her arm and led her towards the bench nearer Dougal, which was the only one in the shade. 'Are you all right?'

'I'm fine. Really I am. Don't fuss.' She sank down on the bench and folded her hands on her swollen belly. Her face was wet with perspiration. 'And who is this?'

'I'm a trespasser, I'm afraid,' Dougal said. 'I really must apologize, Mrs Sutcombe.' He waved at the building beside him and plunged on with desperate fluency. 'Someone mentioned this, and I had to see it for myself. Your husband was just about to send me about my business.'

Georgie dropped the camera on the bench and glanced at Dougal, then down at his wife.

'It is interesting, isn't it?' she said, looking doubtfully at the façade. 'People are always going on about it. They say it's about a hundred years older than the house.'

'Most unusual,' Dougal said quickly, sensing that Georgie was trying to interrupt. 'A combination of ice house and prospect tower?'

'Yes – it's not just a folly. We still use it as a summer house. Grade One listed unfortunately, which means it *eats* money.'

Georgie cleared his throat. 'As I was saying, this is private property.'

'Yes, I must go.' Dougal picked up the camera case, which brought him close to Georgie. 'Sorry again.'

Mrs Sutcombe dabbed her face with a paper handkerchief.

'There's a short cut to the main gate,' Georgie said. 'Frank will show you.'

'There's no need. I—'

'It's no trouble.'

Dougal accepted the inevitable. This time he and Franky-Boy walked along the edge of the woods towards the gap-toothed avenue of copper beeches marking the drive. It was not very far. Dougal guessed that on their way from the lodge to the tower Franky-Boy had taken him on a roundabout route through the wood to avoid the risk of their being seen from the house.

Dougal waited until they were out of earshot of the Sutcombes. 'If you try anything with that knife of yours, I'm going to scream,' he said. 'And scream and scream. I guarantee Mrs Sutcombe will hear. That's not what Georgie wants, is it? He doesn't want her worried. She's in a delicate state of health.'

'Shut up,' Franky-Boy said – in a whisper, which suggested he was alive to the danger of disturbing Mrs Sutcombe.

They walked in silence until they reached the railings which ran parallel to the drive. Dougal glanced back. The tower was still in sight. Georgie was sitting beside his wife with his arm round her shoulders.

'You can go now,' Dougal said.

'No.'

'Then I'll scream. And remember, she can still see you.'

Franky-Boy's head swayed from side to side. A way of saying no, Dougal wondered? Or merely a sign of confusion?

'Use your head,' Dougal advised. 'It's too dangerous to do anything but let me go. There are two reasons why Georgie wants me safely off the premises. Safely means undamaged, by the way. Reason one: Mrs Sutcombe has seen me. Reason two: any excitement could give her a miscarriage, which would probably be fatal at her age. So don't be a fool.'

'I'm not,' said Franky-Boy, aggrieved.

Dougal climbed over the fence. 'He just wants you to make sure I leave,' he said. 'There's no other explanation.'

He crossed the line of beeches and reached the drive. On his left, the chimney of the lodge was visible in a gap between the trees. He stopped and looked back. Franky-Boy was still standing by the fence.

'I'm leaving now,' Dougal said, and waved. 'Bye.'

Franky-Boy raised his arm and waved the Stanley knife. 'Bye,' he whispered.

Dougal knew there was nothing to worry about.

He had phoned first and got the answering machine. Celia's car wasn't in the drive. Besides she had told him yesterday evening that she would be tied up in a series of meetings all day. It was only just after four o'clock, so she shouldn't be back for at least an hour. He had his cover story ready in the unlikely event of anyone challenging him: he was calling to collect some bedding he had left in the loft because the bedbugs had a prior claim on the studio blankets.

Nevertheless he felt a stirring of unease as he let himself into the Kew house. This had less to do with the risk of someone noticing him than with the fact this was Celia's home. He also had a dull ache in the pit of his stomach, which he ascribed to tension.

He turned off the burglar alarm and fetched a black plastic bin-liner from the kitchen. He went upstairs, glancing at the watercolours on the walls and sniffing the smells. These things should have been familiar but they had already acquired an alien quality which meant that he could no longer take them for granted. Just before he reached the first landing he suddenly felt faint: he swayed and had to grip the handrail to stop himself falling.

Delayed reaction, he told himself. Less than three hours ago he had been in that tower waiting for Georgie and Franky-Boy to do something nasty to him. He needed time to recover. There wasn't any time. He forced himself towards the next flight of stairs.

Celia's study filled most of the top floor, but the conversion had left some awkwardly shaped loft space for storage. Dougal found a blanket and an old eiderdown, which he stuffed into the sack. He banged his temple against a purlin. He waited for the pain to subside. It was very hot. The slates sucked in warmth. The bites itched furiously. At last his head began to clear. He carried the sack into Celia's study.

He tried the top drawer of the filing cabinet. It wasn't even locked. Why should she bother? Inside the drawer was a mass of files, discs and papers. There was a blue envelope file on top. It was labelled AUSTERFORD 2000.

It's too easy, Dougal thought; there must be a catch. He opened the file. The papers inside were distributed among four transparent document wallets, their shiny plastic an excellent surface for fingerprints. He sat down at the desk and found himself staring at a photograph in a Perspex holder tucked unobtrusively between the computer and the fax machine. It was a picture of himself with Eleanor on his shoulders; Celia had taken it a couple of years before in the back garden.

He wasn't sure if he had spoken the words aloud: 'I'm doing this for you as much as for me.'

Superficially true; but specious if doing duty was a justification. He was spying on her.

This time he did speak aloud. 'I wouldn't be doing this if I had any alternative.'

But there was an alternative, just as there always had been in the past. He could have told Celia everything he knew and suspected and then asked her what she knew. The problem was, he was so deeply involved that one admission would inevitably lead to another. All roads led back to Miles. Total honesty with others, Dougal told himself, is a social evil and maybe a psychological one too: a form of madness. In this case, he argued, honesty meant damaging himself and those he loved; so perhaps honesty should be downgraded among the virtues and considered as an ethical luxury, a higher form of selfishness.

Now he was here with the file in front of him, his inhibitions abruptly fell away. Excitement gripped him. He wanted the truth as a thirsty man wants water. He examined the wallets one by one, resisting the urge to hurry and carefully preserving the order of the material they contained.

It was all here – correspondence, draft press releases, an outline of promotional strategy, evidence of expenses, plans, photographs and a draft contract between Brassard Prentisse Communications and a company called Austerford Holdings. There was even a short, badly typed document entitled 'Security Parameters: An Overview' and signed 'Harry Vane'. Most illuminating of all, however, were Celia's notes – a series of laconic memoranda to herself. 'Baby due mid-June,' said one. 'NB high blood pressure.' 'Target,' said another, '£5.2m turnover by year 2.'

Kathy Sutcombe had inherited Austerford Hall and what was left of its estate from her first husband, who died in a car crash two years before. He had already obtained outline planning permission to turn part of the park into a golf course. Georgie Sutcombe, however, had far more ambitious plans. These hinged on his perception that the country's population was ageing: there were more retired people than ever before; they lived longer than their forebears and they had much more money at their disposal.

Georgie and his professional advisers had put together what they called 'a programme of phased growth in line with the County Structure Plan'. They envisaged not just a golf course but a complete leisure complex restricted to the over-fifties; and this plan interlocked with a far more lucrative and more complicated scheme to use Austerford and its environs as a gigantic machine to milk the elderly of their surplus wealth. There would be a helipad, a luxury hotel in the Hall itself, office facilities, independent flats and maisonettes, time-share apartments and sheltered housing, and cadres of medical, para-medical and domestic staff. There would also be large-scale landscape development, which would include the creation of two lakes.

Austerford Holdings had held informal talks with the relevant planning authorities, who raised no objections in principle to the scheme. However, the Sutcombes were actively avoiding publicity at this stage because of the need to acquire neighbouring properties vital to the development. Several sets of negotiations were in progress. A premature announcement would drive up prices to unrealistic levels and perhaps lead to local opposition.

Moreover no such announcement could be made until Austerford Holdings had put outside finance in place. This should not take long because a Japanese bank was willing to provide much of the initial capital required for the project; the deal had been agreed in broad outline, and the lawyers were working out the details. These should be finalized at the end of July; as part of the arrangement, Mrs Sutcombe would formally transfer ownership of the Austerford estate from herself to Austerford Holdings. Georgie must have come up with a very attractive proposal, Dougal thought: in these straitened times, even the wealthiest bank would think twice about investing in property development.

Celia's campaign had two aims: first a 'hearts and minds' offensive to win over any doubters among the local population; and second a long-running and probably international promotion to attract the elderly and their wealth to Austerford. On the one hand her proposals made much of the economic and indeed ecological benefits the project would bring to the area; on the other, they made Austerford sound like a veritable Shangri-La within easy reach of London and Luton Airport.

Dougal made a note of the bank and the officials Georgie was dealing with; he also scribbled down the name of the solicitors who were acting for Austerford Holdings – a firm in Lincoln's Inn. He returned the folders to the file and put the file back in the filing cabinet.

For a few seconds he stared at the blank screen of the computer. It was such a grubby business. Not just his own job, his own life – he was used to the accommodations which these forced on him. What disturbed him was this unlicensed insight into Celia's work: Georgie Sutcombe and the bank wanted to make as much money as they could; and Celia had been hired to put an acceptable face on their greed. Like himself, though on a smaller scale, she was willing to take liberties with the truth in return for money. Were her company, this house and the possibility of private education for Eleanor really so important to her?

He picked up the phone and punched in a number. It was answered at the second ring.

'Yes.'

'It's William Dougal, Mrs Provender. No news, I'm afraid.'

There was a silence at the other end of the line. Then, faintly, he heard Mr Provender's voice raised in song: 'Thou art lost and gone for ever, oh my darling Clementine.'

'Are you coping?' he asked.

'It's not one of his good days. And . . . and I keep remembering that this isn't a bad dream.'

'I wish I had some good news,' Dougal said.

'I know you do.'

'Oh, my darling,' Stanley Provender sang, 'oh my darling . . .'

'Tell me,' she went on, 'and please be absolutely honest, don't try and spare my feelings: do you think Miles is all right? Do you think he'll ever come back?'

Down by the river at Putney the early evening sun was still unbearably hot. When he was left alone for a moment, Dougal scratched his bites at first surreptitiously and then with complete abandon.

He was sitting on the balcony of Joan's flat, whose rent he suspected was paid by Hanbury or more likely by Custodemus. As he scratched, he watched the traffic inching over the bridge. The air shimmered with exhaust fumes. Straight lines became curves and hard objects looked soft. Squat manikins fought their way on and off red buses; the British were losing the art of the queue.

The water sparkled in the sunshine. Pleasure boats bobbed at their buoys. A passenger boat chugged downstream towards Westminster. Two eights moved like stick insects towards the boathouses on the other side the river.

An anarchic twittering, rendered strangely soothing by distance, rose from this mass of activity: it was a compound of engine noises, horns, the screams of seagulls, shouts, the cooing of pigeons and the wails of sirens. Emergency lights were flashing on both carriageways: someone had fallen ill, someone's house was on fire, someone had been robbed, someone was dead.

'*Et voilà, monsieur.*'

Hanbury came through the french windows from the living room carrying a tray, which he placed with a flourish on the table beside the chairs. There was a second glass of mineral water for Dougal, and Hanbury had another bottle of a South American lager that cost the earth and tasted of nothing in particular. The mineral water had cubes of ice and two fresh slices of lemon, because Hanbury believed such details counted for something in the constant battle to maintain standards. Also on the tray was a copy of the evening paper.

Hanbury lay back in the chair with a sigh of pleasure. His hair was still dark and shiny from the shower. He took a long swallow of lager and smiled at Dougal. He looked like someone who had discovered the secret of happiness. But appearances were probably deceptive. They usually were.

'Yes – Osmond-MacDonald,' Hanbury said, as though there had been no interruption in their conversation. 'No reason why you should remember. It's not as if you're in the same line of work or connected with one of the victims. Nasty business, but it wasn't front-page stuff by any means. The sums of money weren't large enough. Considered in isolation, I mean – the aggregate must have been well into seven figures. And there wasn't any real *drama* about it, either: it never came to court. Osmond just disappeared.'

'Do you think he was tipped off?'

'It's always possible. Or he may have been one of those rare people who know that enough is as good as a feast.'

Hanbury preened himself unobtrusively. He lit a cigarette and, as an afterthought, offered the packet to Dougal, who shook his head.

'He'd never get away with it now,' Hanbury went on. 'What with the Financial Services Act and so on. But he was clever. He didn't just set up a false identity as Osmond. He set up another one as Trotwood. That's real attention to detail. Even Joan didn't know who he really was. One can't help admiring him.' There was a pause. Hanbury said sharply, 'Are you OK?'

'What?' Dougal's attention had wandered back to the hordes on the bridge. He felt increasingly sleepy. Hanbury's voice was acting on him like a hypnotist's.

'I don't feel I have all your attention.'

'Sorry. Was Franky-Boy involved with Osmond-MacDonald?'

'Possibly. Though not, I would think, in any position requiring intellectual finesse.'

'He panicked today. Over-reacted when Vane told him I was asking questions. I got the impression Georgie wasn't pleased.'

'Don't underrate him,' Hanbury said. 'The two of them are very close. And brains are all very well but it's never wise to underestimate brawn. Franky-Boy's good at hurting people. Joan said that when he was at the villa he used to keep his hand in by experimenting on stray cats.'

'He's not going to experiment on me.'

'Of course not. You won't have to see either of them ever again. I guarantee it.'

They both drank. Dougal could see the *Evening Standard* on the edge of his field of vision. It had the dishevelled look of a newspaper that has been looked at and then tossed aside. Dougal needed an act of will not to pick it up, and another act of will not to blurt out questions.

'You shouldn't have any problems at all,' Hanbury said. 'Kathy Sutcombe's condition can only have the effect of increasing our leverage. If I were you, though, I'd muddy the waters by declaring an interest. You could say you're acting for Mary Jane Filkins.'

'Who's she?'

'Was, dear boy, was. I'm told that Mrs Filkins has gone to join Mr Filkins. And not before time: I don't think her last few years on this earth were particularly happy ones. They stuffed her in one of those old people's homes. Out of sight, out of mind, eh? No kith nor kin, you see. Until now. You could be her long-lost second cousin once removed. Perhaps you combine a passion for genealogy with a passion for justice.'

'James – do you mind keeping it simple?'

'You look rather flushed.'

'It's because we're sitting in the sun.'

'Darling,' Hanbury said.

Dougal looked up, shocked for a split second by his apparently enhanced place in the hierarchy of Hanbury's affections. There was Joan looking down at them with a glass of what looked like whisky in her hand. He wondered how much she had heard. She was wearing a short blue towelling robe and her plaster cast. Her damp hair was lank and unbrushed, and Dougal glimpsed the dark roots. He was shocked by her face: all the good humour and charm, even the prettiness, had vanished like a layer of make-up.

'Come and sit down,' Hanbury said.

'I'll stand.' She swallowed the contents of the glass in one go. 'What's this about the bitch's *condition*?'

'Ah – William says she's due to have a baby in about a month's time.' Hanbury got up and took her hand. 'You must be strong, dearest.'

'So when did Georgie find out he's going to be a daddy?'

'That we don't know – not for sure. But I've had some checking done at St Catherine's House. He and Kathy were married in December.'

There was a silence. The colour drained away behind Joan's tan. She pushed past Hanbury, put down her tumbler on the table and picked up the wallet of photographs. She skimmed through the prints.

'I've never seen him without a beard,' she said, letting the photographs fall in a glistening heap on the table. 'And Franky-Boy used to have one too. He always liked to have what Georgie had. He wanted me too . . . You know something, William? When he married that woman, Georgie was still living with me. The bastard.' She glared at Dougal. 'Is she beautiful?'

Dougal thought of Kathy Sutcombe's smile. He looked at Joan and said, 'No. But she seemed pleasant enough.' He hesitated, searching for a way to offer comfort. 'She owns the Austerford estate and she's also got her first husband's corset factory.'

'Corsets.' Joan's voice wobbled. 'A rich fat widow.'

'Another thing,' Hanbury interposed smoothly. 'I'm almost certain that Sutcombe is Georgie's real name. You see what that means?'

'This time he wants to settle down,' Joan said. 'So the Austerford 2000 thing's entirely legit. Right?'

Hanbury gave a nod. 'Which makes him all the more

vulnerable. And my researchers also checked for siblings. There's a younger brother, apparently. Francis.'

'Doesn't surprise me. He offered me to Franky-Boy when he gave me the push. No joke intended. Baby brother's reward for meritorious service – my consolation prize.' Joan was breathing hard and talking fast. 'When I said piss off to both of them, Georgie said well your time's up, number nine. So I chucked a glass at him. And he told Franky-Boy to—'

Hanbury hugged her, and his shoulder cut off the flow of words. She was shaking. He was murmuring to her, but Dougal couldn't hear what he was saying. He had not thought that Hanbury was capable of being so gentle.

Joan pulled herself away. 'I'm all right now,' she snapped, clinging to his arm.

Hanbury looked at her face and nodded. 'Good.'

'When are you going to do it?'

'Tonight,' Hanbury said. 'That is, William will. No point in dawdling, eh? Georgie knows that something's up. We don't want to give him time to make a counter-move.'

Dougal said, 'Can he pay that much? And so quickly?'

Joan sniffed. 'He can always raise money, love. Just a phone call away. He's got these little offshore nest eggs all over the shop. Regular Easter bunny, Georgie is. I want another drink.'

'Let me get it, darling.'

'No. The exercise will do me good.'

Joan stumped into the living room, the cast thudding on the carpet. Hanbury sat down again, twisting in his chair so he could watch her. Dougal heard a bottle chinking on glass.

'Phew,' he said softly to Dougal. 'A sore subject.'

'Kathy?'

'It's not quite as simple as it seems. When Franky-Boy threw her off the balcony, Joan was pregnant. She lost the baby, of course. I think she got pregnant on purpose. She hoped it would persuade Georgie to – ah – regularize her position.'

A door slammed.

Hanbury wrinkled his forehead. 'The kitchen. Oh dear. It

looks like dinner *chez nous* tonight. Joan's not a great one for cooking – only does it when she's feeling low.'

'How did she find out about Osmond-MacDonald?'

'She says that Georgie left the safe open one night when he was a little the worse for wear. She had enough time to see a bundle of newspaper cuttings. Enough time to read a few headlines.'

'Talking of headlines,' Dougal said. He touched the *Evening Standard.* 'Is there anything in today?'

Hanbury smiled. 'About what they call the Slough Escort corpse? No, not in there. But I had a word with the investigating officer this morning—'

'What? For God's sake—'

'Don't worry. We have a perfectly legitimate interest in that Custodemus is one of the creditors of the site's owners. I had a memo from our legal department – they wanted to find out if this business would delay the bankruptcy proceedings.'

'So there's news? The police have found something?'

'It's not official. I understand they're keeping it under their hat for the time being.'

Hanbury paused for a sip of lager. Dougal watched his hands clenching on his lap.

'Yes . . .' Hanbury belched softly. 'Excuse me. Yes, the police found traces of cannabis at the scene of the fire. The place is very near Heathrow Airport, and they think it may have been a major depot for a drug distribution network. Who would have thought it, eh?'

He beamed at Dougal, who thought that this was a latter-day version of the parable of the loaves and fishes. Hanbury had taken perhaps a gram of hash from Dougal's mantelpiece and miraculously expanded it into evidence of large-scale drug smuggling.

'They've also had an anonymous tip-off about the killing.' Without warning Hanbury's accent lurched north of the border, from London to Edinburgh and beyond. 'Sounded like a Scot, probably a Glaswegian.' He reverted to Received Pronunciation. 'According to the caller, the body belonged to a potential informer, as yet unidentified, working for a competing organization. The police tell me that heroin's at the bottom of it. So it looks like it's turned into one of those cases where they have a pretty good idea what's happened but very little actual evidence. A professional job. All they can do is hope that eventually someone else will turn informer.' Hanbury's eyes met Dougal's. Hanbury smiled. 'But I rather doubt they will.'

'So that's it, is it?' Dougal said.

'It certainly seems so. All's well that ends well. And in half an hour's time you'll have finished too.'

'Longer than that. I've got to return the camera.'

'A mere detail. I don't think anyone would notice if you didn't. But that reminds me: have you phoned Mrs Provender today? We must keep in touch with such a valued client.'

'Yes. I promised I'd go and talk to the neighbours this evening.'

'Splendid. Leave no stone unturned. I know I can rely on you. As indeed you can on me.'

'Thank you,' Dougal said mechanically, because he felt it was expected.

'My pleasure, William. That's what friends are for.' Hanbury got up. 'If you'll excuse me, I'll just see how Joan is.' He glanced at Dougal and frowned. 'What is it now?'

'Georgie thinks I'm Miles,' Dougal burst out. 'Isn't it bloody absurd?'

'May I speak to Mr George Sutcombe please?' Dougal asked.

'Could he possibly call you back?' Kathy Sutcombe said. 'He's talking to someone – I could take a message.'

'It's rather urgent, I'm afraid. This is Chief Inspector Brian MacDonald, Bedford CID.'

'Oh dear – yes, of course, I'll fetch him right away. May I say what it's about?'

'Filkins.'

'Sorry? What?'

'Not what, madam. Who. Tell him it's about M. J. Filkins.'

'Nothing serious, I hope?'

Dougal left the question unanswered from necessity rather than policy. He needed to cover the mouthpiece of the phone. The PA system at Earl's Court had come to life and might betray the fact that he was phoning not from Bedford but from a London underground station. The announcer warned passengers not to leave their baggage untended.

'Well, anyway – I'll get him now,' Mrs Sutcombe said, and she gave a nervous giggle.

Dougal actually heard her walking away from the phone – slap, slap, slap, slap, with the sound diminishing at each step. He visualized down-at-heel slippers with leather soles walking slowly down a long, tiled corridor. He saw the shapeless brown dress and the heavy movements, as if underwater, of a weary woman in the last month of a difficult pregnancy. The sound of her feet was gradually swamped by the noises of the station concourse.

For the third time, Dougal checked that he had his notes ready and that his phonecard wasn't on the verge of running out. He strained to hear Georgie's footsteps approaching.

'Yes,' Georgie said suddenly in Dougal's ear.

'All you need do is listen,' Dougal said. 'A file has been prepared on you. This is an outline of its contents. At present you call yourself Sutcombe, but you have also used the name Osmond. As Georgie Osmond, you ran Osmond-MacDonald, a firm of investment consultants operating along the south coast. Your partner, Brian MacDonald, was just a convenient fiction adding weight to the letterhead. You specialized in elderly clients with declining incomes whose main assets were their homes. You liked childless widows especially. You increased their incomes, often dramatically, by rescheduling their investments and releasing the equity tied up in their homes.'

'This has got nothing to do with me.'

'Then you disappeared. "Building up a new client base in the Midlands" – that was the formula. No one worried because the cheques were still coming in once a month. Then five months later they stopped and people started going to the police.'

'Look, Miles. You've got the wrong person. Let me tell you—'

'Shut up.'

Suddenly a man began to gabble unintelligibly on the PA system. Dougal pressed on. It didn't really matter if Georgie guessed he was phoning from London.

'Unless you co-operate fully, copies of the file will be sent to your wife, and to Takashi Hasegawa. I'm sure you've met Mr Hasegawa. He's assistant general manager at the Asahi Bank, isn't he? One of his responsibilities is overseeing project finance. Further copies will be sent to the police and to representatives of the media. All this can be avoided if you make a one-off payment of four hundred thousand pounds sterling within twenty-four hours.'

'You off your head or something? Touch of the sun?'

'The money should be paid into the account of Brian MacDonald at the Windward Credit Bank, Georgetown, Grand Cayman. Don't forget, Georgie: MacDonald, Windward Credit. They operate a twenty-four-hour service for deposits. The account number is 130341. Easy to remember: it's your birthday. Not your real birthday – Osmond's.'

Georgie started to laugh, which was all wrong.

But Dougal, acting under instructions, put the phone down. A West Indian girl moved forward to take the handset from him before he had even retrieved his phonecard. He realized that in the last few seconds a small crowd had gathered behind him. For an instant of terror he thought he had done his blackmailing in front of an audience of at least a dozen people. He scanned their faces but none of them seemed in the least interested in him since he had relinquished the phone.

A woman with clearer diction began to repeat the announcement over the PA system. There had been bomb alerts at Paddington and Hammersmith; both stations were now closed; delays would occur throughout the system and passengers were advised if possible to find alternative means of transport.

12

For humanitarian reasons, Dougal hoped that the bomb warn-
ings would turn out to be hoaxes – bizarre but bloodless
contributions to a political process, a war or perhaps a vendetta.
Those responsible for such gestures seemed curiously incapable
of clarifying their aims and objectives. Dougal thought that
what they needed was a good, hungry public relations company.
Brassard Prentisse Communications, perhaps.

He went out into Earl's Court Road. Passengers rushed in
and out of the station in search of information and trains. For
people who weren't trying to be somewhere else, life was going
on much as normal. Near the entrance, a busker was playing
an old Beatles hit on a guitar with only four strings; coiled
round his feet was a wiry, alert little mongrel. A little further
along the road two middle-aged men sat comfortably, their
legs outstretched on the pavement, with a grubby rucksack
and a Selfridges carrier bag between them. One was drinking
sherry, the other the strongest lager on the market, and they
were talking animatedly.

The busker's song was called 'Love Is All You Need'. Dougal
dropped a pound coin in the hat beside the dog.

'It's not on, I said to her,' the sherry-drinker was remarking
to his colleague as Dougal approached, 'my body's not for sale.'
He looked up at Dougal. 'Spare change, guv?' Unlike the good
Samaritan Dougal passed by. 'So she said, it's not your body
I want, it's your mind.'

An air of unreality had descended on the city. This was one
of the usual effects of a bomb or hoax – unless you were directly
affected by a blast, the distinction was immaterial because many

of the consequences were identical. In either case people were jolted temporarily out of the comfortable numbness of their routines, with the result that they saw their surroundings clearly, often for the first time since the last bomb alert.

According to London Transport, which was doing its best to keep everyone informed, trains had stopped running in the centre of the city and in most of the western suburbs. Many British Rail trains had also been cancelled. Dougal walked up to Kensington High Street and turned left. The road was clogged with cars, a situation that demonstrated yet again that the term 'rush hour' should be taken ironically. He soon discovered that buses had become a dwindling species and vacant taxis almost extinct. He plodded westwards. Tourists stood on street corners looking understandably worried and directing questions at anyone in uniform.

A double-decker had stopped at traffic lights. Dougal squeezed on board and eavesdropped on his neighbours' conversations. As usual people were mainly interested in such matters as whether the tubes were open west of Turnham Green and the precise route of the Number 73 bus. Whether from selfishness or common sense, they domesticated the bombs, real or imaginary, and therefore cut them down to size.

Dougal got off at Hammersmith. Both tube stations at the Broadway were closed so he went on into King Street. As he walked Dougal made a commendable effort to ignore his tiredness and his impatience, and to enjoy the exercise and the evening air.

For this was the beginning of the end of his troubles. He should be feeling happy, or at least hugely relieved. Now Miles would stay away for ever. Miles and miles away. Dougal had paid his dues to Hanbury. Now he could get on with his new life. Now he could try to deal with what he hoped were lesser problems, starting with the bedbugs and working upwards to those associated with higher life forms.

King Street became Chiswick High Road. By now Dougal's glow from healthy exercise had degenerated into overheated weariness. His shoes were new, and they weren't designed for serious walking; the left one pinched his toes. He made short detours to check the stations just off his route, only to find that they were still closed.

He walked on, more slowly now, regretting the consequences of trying to be too clever. After going to Kew to pry in Celia's files, he had driven down the road to Richmond and left the Sierra in a car park near the station; he had picked up the film he had left to be developed and caught the tube into town for his meeting with Joan and Hanbury. It had seemed a good idea at the time: he knew he would have to return to Richmond for his second visit to Miles's flat, and the tube offered a relatively pleasant alternative to driving in London in the rush hour.

But the bomb alerts had changed everything. Their effects rippled through Dougal's life and forward into the far future. It was because of them that he found himself walking towards Turnham Green underground station at a quarter to eight on a hot May evening. It was because of the bombs, real or imaginary, that he chanced to walk past the office block housing Brassard Prentisse Communications. So in a way it was because of the bombs that James Hanbury eventually changed his mind.

'What are you doing here?'

Celia sounded angry, which surprised Dougal because when he left her yesterday evening they had been on friendlier terms than for some time. She and Hugo Brassard were standing between her Volvo and his Rover in the parking area in front of the entrance. They had been talking, with their heads close together, when he first saw them. Now they were both staring at him.

Dougal stopped. 'Why shouldn't I be here?'

Suddenly her face became sharper, almost desperate. 'Have you got news about Miles? Bad news? Is that why you've come?'

'No. There's no news. I'm looking for a train.'

Brassard sighed. 'You won't find one in Turnham Green.'

His face was an unhealthy colour – white tinged with a greeny-yellow – and he had propped up his long, pinstriped body against the side of his car. 'Not in either direction.'

'But where are you trying to get to?' Celia asked.

'Richmond.' Dougal felt anger bubbling beneath the surface. 'My car's there.'

'I really think these people should be more thoughtful,' Brassard was saying, presumably with the terrorists in mind. 'Causing all this inconvenience to innocent people is not the way to win support, is it?'

'Richmond?' Celia said.

'Yes.' Dougal's anger gave off a jet of steam. 'I'm meant to be looking for Miles, remember?'

Brassard was pursuing his own line of thought. 'The bombs are meant to be in the centre. I can't understand why they should affect the trains out here.'

Celia looked at Brassard. Dougal couldn't see her face. He would have liked to apologize but he couldn't find the appropriate formula for the occasion. Adding to his confusion was the feeling that he was looking so hard for Miles that one day he might actually find him.

'Sheer incompetence,' Brassard was saying. 'You wouldn't get that in the private sector. If I were responsible, I'd—'

'So what are you going to do?' Celia interrupted. 'Try and find a taxi?'

'You'll be lucky,' Dougal said. 'Where are you going?'

Brassard brought his mind to bear on the immediate problem. 'My sister's. It's her night for the operatic society, and I promised I'd collect my niece – she's in a debate at school this evening. She's developing into quite a talented public speaker.' For an instant he lifted his head and smiled proudly, and Dougal glimpsed the ghost of the old, smug-faced Hugo Brassard. Then the forehead puckered into a tangle of corrugations. 'I could try a bus, I suppose.'

'There aren't many of those around either,' Dougal said. 'Why can't you drive?'

'Wretched car won't start. That's what comes of buying British. Celia, I don't suppose you'd lend me yours?'

'No. I'll need it myself.'

'If you could give me a lift . . .?'

'I'm *busy*, Hugo. I won't be leaving here for at least a couple of hours.' She glanced at her watch. 'And I promised I'd phone Mrs Provender.'

'Oh dear.'

'You'll have to phone the school and leave a message,' Celia said in a voice she had developed for use on Eleanor. 'Either a friend will take her home or they'll get her a taxi. Then you can phone the AA, and they'll send someone round to sort out the car. And while you're waiting there's plenty to do in the office. If you're lucky you may be able to get to the school before the end of the debate.'

'I hate to disappoint her if there's any chance . . . But I suppose you're right. One must be sensible.'

Celia's eyes met Dougal's. In happier times a spark of amusement might have jumped between them because they used to share a joke about Brassard's desire to be sensible. It seemed to Dougal that now there was nothing left to share. Except—

'When are you collecting Eleanor?' Dougal said.

'The weekend, some time. I don't know.'

'I'll fetch her if you want.'

'We'll see,' she said. 'It all depends on what happens here. I'm going to be very tied up.'

'I appreciate that.'

She appeared not to register the sarcasm in his voice. 'Are you actually going to Miles's flat?'

'Yes,' Dougal said, shifting his weight from one aching foot to the other; he wished she wouldn't keep bringing the conversation back to Miles Provender.

'But you've already searched it pretty thoroughly, haven't you?'

'Yes, last night. I told you. Why?'

'It's just that one of his Custodemus files is missing. I

127

wondered if it was in his briefcase or something. Could you have a look?'

'His briefcase?'

'In fact it's a sort of shoulder bag with a detachable strap. Light brown leather. Didn't you see it?'

'No. I'll have a look if you want.'

'I suppose he might have taken it with him,' Brassard interrupted, his eyes gleaming. 'It's very sturdy and quite a convenient size – big enough for a change of clothes. Any clue's worth following up. Don't you agree, William?'

Dougal ignored the question. He disliked being told how to do his job as much as anyone else did, even when the job was a fiction. 'What does the file look like?' he asked Celia.

'Probably one of those envelope folders. You know the sort. We all use them here.'

Dougal nodded. He had been examining the contents of such a file a few hours earlier. 'He might have left the bag in Thricehurst.'

Celia shook her head. 'I'm almost sure he had it last week. And I don't think he's been down to Thricehurst since the weekend before. But I'll check.'

'Go gently,' Dougal said. 'I talked to Mrs Provender this afternoon. She's having a difficult day.'

Celia and Brassard exchanged glances.

'Aren't we all?' Celia said.

Simultaneously Brassard burst out, 'That could make things tricky, couldn't it? When you talk to her, Celia, you must stress that we think of Miles as a friend not just a colleague. And make a point of asking if there's anything we can do. Absolutely anything.'

'Like find her son?' Dougal suggested. 'Or get her husband a brain transplant?'

Celia's lips twisted with distaste. Brassard almost whinnied with embarrassment.

'It's the truth, isn't it?' Dougal said, looking from one to the other. 'That's all she wants. And all you want is her money.'

★   ★   ★

A few hundred yards down Chiswick High Road, a warm, yeasty smell wafted on to the pavement from an open doorway. Dougal's resolution cracked.

He went into the pub. The bar was set against the rear wall and shaped like a horseshoe, and around it was a cavernous room filled with pale faces, gleaming glasses and wisps of smoke.

It took him a while to get served. He thought the barmaid looked strangely at him. Inside he was still shaking with anger, and maybe a trace of it showed in his face. Righteous anger, he told himself firmly; and then a cooler part of his mind pointed out that angry people almost always tried to justify their anger by telling themselves it was righteous; whereas more often than not anger had its deep and irrational roots in fear, stupidity and selfishness.

He changed a ten-pound note and took his pint and sandwich over to a table near the pay phone. His mouth was dry and his stomach felt knotted. He wanted to sleep for a thousand years and wake in another world.

The sandwich tasted of substances like sawdust, plastic and blotting paper. But the beer was good, perhaps too good. If one pint was good, then two would be better; and on his way back to the studio he could pop into another pub for a third.

Going to Richmond tonight now seemed a stupid idea. What was the point in pushing himself so hard? Miles wasn't going anywhere so continuing the investigation could wait till tomorrow. He could phone Mrs Provender and explain about the bombs – she would understand the delay. He needed rest. The events of the week had left him feeling like a zombie. And the week wasn't over yet.

He drank half of the beer and went to the phone. There were two calls he needed to make. He thumbed a pound coin into the slot and dialled the first number from memory.

'Hello,' Celia's stepmother whispered in his ear.

Dougal glanced at the clock over the bar. 'Margaret? It's William. How are you?'

'Eleanor's in bed, asleep. I told you before—'

'I'm sorry. I didn't have time to ring before.'

'Have you thought about what I said?'

'In general I'm sure you're right.' Dougal knew this was usually a safe line to take with Margaret Prentisse. There was a pause as he cast his mind over his last conversation with her – on Monday evening just before the drunken dinner with Hanbury and Joan at the Royal Commonwealth Institute. 'Children need all the sleep they can get. But Eleanor's always seemed to need less than other—'

'I wasn't talking about Eleanor's sleep routine, not this time. I'm talking about you and Celia.' Margaret forgot to whisper. 'Eleanor needs a mummy *and* a daddy.'

'I agree.'

'I know it's an old-fashioned view but that doesn't mean it's wrong. And here's another old-fashioned view. I think Celia's getting too tied up with her work. I know it's important, that it brings in the bread and butter, but a little girl needs her mummy. That's even more important.'

Dougal cleared his throat. 'The trouble is—'

'Listen, William. Eleanor's started having nightmares. Last night she wet her bed, which is something she hasn't done for years.'

'But what's wrong with her?' Dougal said.

'If you ask me, it's because you and Celia are separating. I don't mind your dumping her on me – I love having her here. But Eleanor doesn't see it like that.'

'Then how does she see it?'

'She thinks she's being punished, of course, and that you and Celia don't want her. She thinks your silly squabbles are all her fault.'

13

'Miles who?' said the man who opened the door of the third flat. He was wearing a towel and nothing else.

'Provender,' Dougal said. 'He lives upstairs in number nine.'

'Never heard of him. Sorry.'

The door began to close. In the background another man was talking. The voice sounded familiar. The words stopped, to be replaced by a burst of big-band music. The name of the tune hovered on the edge of Dougal's memory.

'You must have seen him around. Early thirties, dark hair, about your height. Drives a Cavalier.'

'The one in the car park? Purple?'

'That's it.'

The music sounded like Duke Ellington. Inspector Coleford's chief recreation was listening to his extensive collection of 78s and long-playing records by Duke Ellington; this activity sent him into a trance which often produced one of those flashes of intuition on which his forensic reputation was founded. The series was shown on Monday nights, not Wednesday, so the man must be watching it on video.

'Yeah, I've seen the car – it's there now – but I've never seen him, or not that I know of. All right?'

The door shut with a click.

'Thank you for your time,' Dougal said. He walked a few yards along the passage and rang the bell of number four.

He had come to Richmond this evening after all; fortunately the tubes were running again. His change of mind was due largely to Margaret Prentisse, who had made him feel so guilty that the beer had turned sour in his mouth. At present there

was nothing he could do to help Eleanor. Fulfilling his obliga-
tions, if that was the right word, to Mrs Provender had seemed
marginally preferable to going back to the studio: it might lessen
the load of guilt if only by a fraction. Besides he wanted to
return the camera, which he had collected from the boot of his
car on his way to the flats. He had a superstitious feeling that
Miles's camera, or indeed any of Miles's possessions, could
only bring him bad luck.

By the time Dougal had rung eight of the twelve doorbells
he had begun to feel that it was just as well that he was not really
looking for Miles Provender. One of the flats appeared to be
untenanted. At three he drew a blank: no one answered the door,
though in at least one case he heard movements inside. Elsewhere
he found someone at home who was willing to talk to him. One
was ruder than the man in number three, two were more polite.
But none of them admitted to knowing what Miles looked like.

Eight flats down, three more to go: these were on the top
floor of the block; one flat was beside Miles's, and the other
two on the opposite side of the landing.

The owner of the first turned out to be a very young man
posing as a middle-aged one. Instead of talking on the doorstep,
he ushered Dougal into his living room, which in shape was
the mirror image of Miles's, and offered him a chair. Dougal
sat down and looked quickly round the room. There were several
bookcases stuffed with paperbacks. Reproductions of well-
known Impressionist paintings hung on the walls. His host had
been playing chess with his personal computer. A Telemann
violin concerto ebbed and flowed in the background. Dougal
asked if he knew Miles.

'In a manner of speaking, yes. We're neighbours.'

'Do you see much of him?'

'No, we have very little contact, I'm afraid,' the young man
drawled, stroking a patch of fluffy fair hair on his upper lip. 'I
asked him in for a glass of sherry once, him and his girlfriend.
Just trying to be civil, you know. That was in March some time
– I'd just moved in. But he made some excuse.'

'His girlfriend?'

'Yes.' The young man turned pink around the edges. 'They aren't living together. But she turns up every now and then.'

Dougal felt sick. 'What's she like?'

'Rather attractive, actually. Good figure. But I've only seen her once or twice. Sometimes I hear them – the walls aren't that thick.' The man's Adam's apple bobbed up and down. 'I think she wears glasses. But surely you've talked to her already?'

'Oh yes,' Dougal said, and pretended to make a note. 'Just checking. Between ourselves, we have to be very careful in my job where girlfriends are concerned. Sometimes it turns out that there's more than one. You understand?'

The young man tried to respond with a man-to-man leer. He turned a darker shade of pink.

'Any idea where he might have gone?' Dougal asked. 'Or why?'

'No, none at all.' By now the drawl had been forgotten, and the words came out in spurts. 'To be honest, he's always seemed a bit – well, unfriendly. I mean I thought he might ask me in for a drink or a cup of coffee. But he hasn't.'

'Maybe he will.' Dougal shut his notebook and stood up. 'Thank you very much for your help.'

There was a certain comfort in activity, even this meaningless charade he was performing for Hanbury and Mrs Provender. He rang the bell of one of the flats opposite. A short, dark-haired woman came to the door with a napkin in her hand, which perhaps explained why she was brusque to the point of rudeness. Yes, she knew who Miles was; no, she hadn't seen him since Friday evening when she'd glimpsed him walking downstairs with someone, probably a man; yes, she thought he had a girlfriend but she'd never seen her and frankly she thought it was none of her business.

She shut the door in Dougal's face. No one answered when he tried the flat next door. Somewhere a phone was ringing. Dougal walked across the landing. He hadn't needed confirmation that Celia had come here. But he'd got it all the same.

He wanted to hit something or someone very hard. He wanted to cry. He wanted to grow up until he reached a point in his emotional development where these things no longer mattered.

The phone was louder: it was ringing inside Miles's flat. Celia hoping against hope that Miles had returned? Suddenly it seemed vital to know who was calling, and why. Dougal searched all his pockets for the flat keys and found them in the last one. As in dreams, the obstacles multiplied as his urgency increased. He ripped the lining of the pocket as he pulled out the keys. They were the wrong keys – Celia's, not Miles's. He remembered that he had transferred Miles's keys to the camera case to avoid just this sort of confusion.

At last he unlocked the door to Miles's flat. He twisted the handle and pushed. As if this were a signal, the phone stopped ringing. Dougal swore. Dream logic was still in control. According to the same logic, something even worse should now happen.

The door opened a few inches, then stopped. He pushed harder. The door wouldn't budge. It had caught on something. For an instant the dream became reality and reality turned into a nightmare.

Oh Christ, Miles is there – Miles is lying dead in the hall, and they'll know I killed him . . .

Dougal took a step backwards. A pit had suddenly opened up before him. He could almost see it: a well of darkness. If he fell in he would find Miles waiting at the bottom and showing his teeth in a sharklike grin.

But Miles is miles away. The nightmare retreated to bide its time in the back of Dougal's mind. His mouth was dry. He shivered. Just tension and tiredness and worry: nothing more. He hated and feared these reminders that his sanity was fragile, no more than a makeshift barrier against the chaos.

From here he could see that there was something on the floor. He squeezed through the narrow opening into the hall. Wedged between the mat and the bottom of the door was a padded envelope.

His terror dropped away completely, leaving him uncomfortably aware of how ridiculous his behaviour would have seemed to an observer. He bent down and worked the envelope loose. It was addressed to Miles and it was from a mail-order firm which processed and printed films. There was no other post.

You buy a camera. What do you take with your first film? Pictures of your nearest and dearest. Dougal kicked the door shut behind him. He didn't want to open the envelope but he knew that he was going to, that nothing short of physical restraint could stop him.

He went into the living room. Everything looked as it had before. The air was warm and stale. There was a faint underlying smell of decay, which he thought was new. Encouraged by the heat, vegetables were rotting in the kitchen.

The outlines and colours of the furnishings were softer than they had been yesterday. At this time of the evening, the long summer twilight filled the room with shadows. Dougal sat down on the sofa at the end nearer the window. There was still enough light, perhaps too much; part of him didn't want to see too clearly. He ripped open the envelope and pulled out the wallet and the new film inside. He lifted the flap of the wallet. The photographs slipped into his hand.

He was looking into Miles's eyes.

The wallet, the film and the envelope fell to the floor.

The regular features, the tanned skin, the white teeth, the smile: the gorgeous hunk himself. Dougal slid the print to the bottom of the pile. But it was no use. There was Miles again, this time the whole man, as naked as the day he was born but much more hairy and with the beginnings of a very grown-up erection. He was lying on top of the dark blue duvet in the bedroom and still smiling.

What do you take with your first film? Pictures of your nearest and dearest?

Dougal hurriedly moved on to the third print. From deep in his throat came a sound halfway between a grunt and a sob, instantly suppressed.

'Oh God.'

As he spoke a key turned in the lock of the front door.

Reflexes took over. In a second Dougal was on his feet. His conscious mind was a blank. The photographs dropped to the floor and spread face down over the rug like a pack of cards. Nowhere to hide – nowhere to run to. He darted behind the partly open door to the hall.

The front door opened. A moment later it closed softly. Dougal strained to hear. Was that someone else's breathing or his own? It was darker in the hall but the new arrival didn't turn on the light. Hanbury still had Miles's set of keys, but at this moment he should be sampling Joan's cooking at the Putney flat.

Dougal heard a movement in the hall, then silence: he thought that someone had taken a step forward, and then paused to listen. He gritted his teeth so tightly that a shaft of pain shot through his jaw. There was another movement, another silence. He had nothing he could use as a weapon. In the kitchen there must be knives . . .

Someone was breathing – only inches away on the other side of the door. Dougal's nostrils wrinkled. There was a new smell to join the stale air and rotting vegetables, a smell that was much more pleasant and also irritatingly familiar. Footsteps advanced into the room. A figure moved slowly to the window.

Dougal pushed the door shut.

The woman screamed. She whirled round. She raised her arms to ward off attack. The fingers curved into claws.

'Charlotte,' Dougal said.

The scream stopped, unfinished. She parted her lips. Her teeth were clenched, and as white as Miles's. She hissed like a cat at him.

'It's all right. No one will harm you.'

The hissing died away but the mouth stayed open, a red O. Charlotte advanced slowly. Her breathing rasped through the mouth. The fingers flexed as if trying to grip the air.

'It's me. William Dougal.' He hesitated, searching for the right formula. 'Eleanor's dad.'

Charlotte drifted to a halt. Slowly she lowered her arms. She stared blankly at Dougal, her eyes huge behind the glasses. She licked her lips and shut her mouth. She looked quickly round the room. Hope dies hard, Dougal thought: perhaps she thought Miles might be here.

'It's all right,' Dougal said once more. 'No one will hurt you, I promise. Sit down.'

She buckled and almost fell on the sofa. Half sitting, half lying, she looked up at him. The red hair was loose over her shoulders; she wore a short, cotton dress and sandals with heels, both of which helped to show her legs to advantage. The perfume was the one whose traces Dougal had smelled in the hall on his last visit. Charlotte looked over the age of consent. The twilight encouraged the illusion but did not create it. She had done that herself. Outwardly she was no longer a girl. She had turned into a woman. The photograph of her posing naked on Miles's exercise bike had made her physical maturity abundantly clear.

'You were here yesterday?' Dougal said.

She looked at him but gave no sign that she had heard.

'You didn't know Miles was missing until your uncle Hugo told you. Yesterday at his office – you remember? I was there too.'

Charlotte looked away. She began to roll a strand of hair round her forefinger.

'You took the tape from the answering machine because you'd left a message on it. You took Miles's briefcase too. Perhaps you put some of your things in it?'

This time her head moved forward. A nod?

He kept his voice as gentle as he could. 'But you had to come again because you knew Miles had sent off the film. You had to get hold of it before anyone else did. Anyone other than Miles.'

Charlotte made a small wordless noise.

Dougal didn't move. It was growing darker. Streetlights glowed: a yellow fever spread through the city.

'I got here just before you did,' he said. 'The photos were on the mat. I brought them in here. I opened the envelope.'

From the child–woman on the sofa came another quiet sound. An animal in pain.

'I looked at the first photo,' Dougal went on. 'It's a picture of Miles, just his face. But then you came in. I didn't have time to see the other photos, only the first one.' He paused to allow the implications to sink in. 'You understand? I just dropped the photos on the floor. All of them. Look – can you see? By your feet.'

Charlotte slowly straightened herself. Twice she hesitated and glanced at Dougal. She bent down. The hair swung in front of her face. The prints were spread out in an irregular fan shape. Beside them was the wallet they had arrived in.

'They aren't mine,' Dougal said. 'I don't want to see them. You'd better take them.'

She raised her head and looked at him. If you look at a schoolgirl, Dougal thought, you see a schoolgirl; if you look at a woman, you see a woman, in this case quite an attractive one. The trouble was, each description was accurate as far as it went but neither was the whole truth. She was like one of those drawings designed to illustrate perceptual ambiguities: the vase that is also two faces in profile; the rabbit that becomes a duck.

'I suppose they belong to Miles,' he went on. 'But as he isn't here at present, I'm sure he'd want you to look after them.'

Slowly, very slowly, she leant forwards. Her hands crept closer to the floor. The long fingers gently swept the prints together.

'Take the wallet too. The negatives are inside.'

She pushed the photographs into the wallet. Then she sat up, almost briskly. Her back was straight, her legs were together, and she held the wallet with both hands on her lap.

'Why?' she said, so quietly that Dougal hardly heard her. 'Why?'

Because I killed Miles Provender . . .? Was that the answer she wanted? Or was she asking a different question?

He heard rather than saw her crying. She hadn't come alone. She had brought a crowd of problems with her, some of which were now Dougal's.

'How were you planning to get home? Public transport? Is that how you came?'

She sniffed, and nodded. The crying became quieter.

'You know I'm a private detective?' he asked, wondering what had happened to the school debate and Brassard's taxi. 'Mrs Provender and Celia and your uncle have hired me to look for Miles. That's why I'm here. I'm looking for Miles, not for anything else.'

The crying stopped.

'Have you any idea where he is?'

The sobs started again – less violently now.

Dougal waited. He counted the seconds. Five passed, ten, fifteen. He said, 'I think I'd better take you home.'

'No,' she whispered.

'Why not?'

'I want to go by myself.'

'I don't think that's a good idea.'

'I can handle it.'

'I'm sure you can. But it's getting late.'

'You'll tell them,' she said fiercely. 'I know you will. Or you'll tell the police or someone.'

'Why should I do that?'

She waved a hand dismissively. 'Because.'

Dougal counted some more seconds. Five, ten. He moved towards the door. She stared at him. At the door he looked back. She pretended she had been examining her nails.

'I've been checking up on the neighbours,' he said. 'When did they last see Miles – that sort of thing. Some of them were out the first time I called. I'll try them again, OK?'

She said nothing.

'I'll only be a few minutes. But if you want to leave while I'm gone there's nothing to stop you.'

He opened the door. There was a leather bag on the hall

floor – Miles's briefcase, which perhaps contained the Custodemus file that Celia wanted. Charlotte didn't move. In seven or eight years Eleanor could be like that – a silent child–woman on a sofa.

'But if you want to help me find Miles,' he said, 'you'll stay.'

Her head jerked up. 'What do you mean?'

'In a way you know him better than anyone. You may know things you don't realize.'

'Uncle Hugo—'

'This has nothing to do with Uncle Hugo. Or your mother or Celia or anyone else. Just you, me and Miles.'

'Do you think – something's happened to him?'

'Maybe. I think the sooner we find out the better. And if I drive you home we can talk. Nothing you tell me will go any further. I promise. Not unless you want it to.'

'I don't know. I just don't know.'

'You can make up your mind while I'm gone.'

Dougal left the flat. There was less light on the landing; the stairwell was nearly dark, and full of shadows. He was damp with sweat and the cooler air made him shiver. He was so tired he could hardly stand up. First a day at Austerford with Georgie and friends – now an evening that was turning into an emotional switchback. He wondered if Charlotte realized that he could hardly avoid seeing her if she decided to leave without him. The only way to help her was by telling lie after lie. Just so long as he didn't start telling lies to himself. Starting now: was he really trying to help Charlotte for altruistic reasons, or was he covering himself by acting as if this were a genuine case? A bit of both, perhaps. He wasn't sure.

He brushed the unplastered wall searching for a switch. Who would have thought it? Miles seducing a schoolgirl. In life he had seemed such a straightforward person. In death he was becoming increasingly complicated: certainties changed shape and possibilities multiplied. Now he was revealed as a criminal. Having sexual relations with a minor could have earned him a jail sentence. In this particular case, Dougal found it hard to muster the appropriate moral indignation. It seemed probable that Charlotte hadn't objected to being seduced; the only thing upsetting her was Miles's unscheduled absence.

So had Miles been screwing the pair of them, Charlotte and Celia? Or was Charlotte on the way out and Celia on the way in? There was of course a third possibility. For the moment Dougal dared not think about it because he didn't trust his ability to be objective.

His fingertips touched plastic and traced the outline of a time switch. He pressed it down. Light flooded over the landing. He blinked.

Something moved at the head of the stairs. Dougal swung round.

A man ran silently up the last few stairs. He was tall, thin and very fast. His face was a pale and contorted blur that resolved itself into recognizable features as it came nearer.

Dougal blinked. The man moved so quickly towards him that he had no chance to escape. Even if he had been slower, Dougal would have stayed exactly where he was.

Because this time Franky-Boy was carrying a gun.

14

Franky-Boy was wearing jeans and a faded University-of-Chicago sweatshirt beneath a lightweight leather jacket. His feet made no sound as he ran lightly across the concrete floor. He jabbed the muzzle of the small automatic under Dougal's chin. With his free hand he patted Dougal's pockets.

Dougal forced his mouth into a smile. 'Mislaid your Stanley knife?'

Franky-Boy produced a set of keys from Dougal's trousers. As luck would have it, he found the keys for the flat first time. He dangled them in front of Dougal's face.

'Inside.'

'Why?'

The gun forced back Dougal's head until it bumped into the bricks behind him.

'Open the door.'

The Yale lock had engaged automatically. Dougal turned the key. He pushed the door slowly open. Franky-Boy nudged him into the hall. Charlotte hadn't switched on the lights. Presumably she was in the living room. Miles's bag was still on the hall floor. Franky-Boy reached over Dougal's shoulder and pulled the keys from the lock.

'What are you going to do with that gun?' Dougal said loudly. 'Kill me? You'll never—'

Franky-Boy hit him on the side of the head with the butt. Dougal stumbled across the hall. He crashed against the table holding the answering machine. The table fell over with Dougal on top of it. Wood cracked as one of the legs snapped. A sharp, intolerable pain stabbed his cheek. He cried out.

Dougal lay there. The pain subsided to an ache. He wasn't comfortable but he couldn't think what to do next. The phone was still working – he could hear the dialling tone. Something hard was digging into his cheek. He moved his head. It was the model Ferrari. He heard Franky-Boy shutting the door.

'Up.'

Dougal didn't move. A foot thudded into his side. He cried out once more and started to get up. There were a few drops of blood – some on the carpet, some on the phone. Once on his feet he discovered that his knees wouldn't support him. He swayed against the wall.

'If you fire that thing,' Dougal said, 'you do realize it'll make a lot of noise? Think of the neighbours.'

He thought of them himself: neighbours who by and large didn't want to know about each other. Even if they heard a shot they would probably find excuses to ignore it.

Franky-Boy kept the gun on Dougal. He bobbed his head into each room in turn – the bedroom, the bathroom and the living room. He didn't bother to search the place more thoroughly.

Franky-Boy waved the gun at the living-room doorway. 'Shut the door and lean against it. Just there.'

Dougal staggered across the hall and obeyed. His trembling was real but he exaggerated it. Franky-Boy's sneer was his reward. He strained to hear movement on the other side of the door. Half of him hoped that Charlotte would open the window and shout for help. The other half was terrified that she would do just that, which might make Franky-Boy panic and pull the trigger.

Franky-Boy stooped and picked up the phone. The keypad was part of the handset. He straightened up and pushed back the sleeve on his jacket. Dougal glimpsed writing on the skin of his wrist – presumably a phone number.

Dougal's ribs ached where Franky-Boy had kicked them. Lucky it had been the ribs, not the kidneys. He touched his cheek. It felt sticky. He looked at his fingers and saw a smear of blood.

Franky-Boy was trying to punch in the number while holding the gun on Dougal. After a few seconds it dawned on him that this was an unnecessarily cumbersome process. With his eyes on Dougal, he squatted and laid the handset on the floor. Consulting his wrist, he tapped in the number. Between each digit he glanced up at Dougal. There were seven digits, Dougal noticed: so Franky-Boy couldn't be phoning Austerford Hall. He was almost certainly calling an Outer London number.

The phone began to ring at the other end. Franky-Boy, still squatting on his haunches, stared at Dougal with pale blue eyes. As he stared he licked his wrist. The number became a blue blur, and so did the tip of Franky-Boy's tongue.

The ringing stopped.

'It's – it's me. I got him. We're in the flat . . .' Franky-Boy paused. 'No – he's outside still, like you said . . .' Another, shorter pause. 'Right.'

While he was talking, Franky-Boy continued to stare at Dougal. As he said the word 'flat', there was a movement in the doorway of Miles's bedroom. It was on the border of Dougal's range of vision. He saw the movement, but dared not look towards it for fear of his face betraying him. His nails dug into the palms of his hand.

'Right. See you.' Franky-Boy laid the phone on the carpet. A fingertip hovered over the buttons. He looked up at Dougal once more.

'I'm still here,' Dougal said.

As he was speaking there was a rushing of air and thudding of feet. Charlotte erupted from Miles's bedroom. She was holding something in both hands above her head. Her hair rippled behind like a pair of fiery wings. The confined space of the hall seemed full of writhing bodies.

Franky-Boy twisted and raised his head. He started to get up. The gun swung away from Dougal. Franky-Boy changed his mind about standing up and tried to duck instead. He was too late. Charlotte's arms blurred as they swept down in an arc.

She made a sound like a vicious sneeze: 'Ah-*chow*,' with the accent on the second syllable. That was when the blow connected. Miles's cricket bat smacked against Franky-Boy's skull just below the receding hairline. The gun went off. Franky-Boy collapsed in a huddle of limbs on top of the telephone and the remains of the table.

In a second the tiny hall had filled with acrid smoke. Dougal knew he wasn't hit, and Charlotte seemed undamaged. He took a step forward and looked around for the gun. He couldn't see it: Franky-Boy could well be lying on top of it. Had the fool shot himself? Christ, Dougal thought, his mind moving ahead to the next problem: not another body on his hands?

He glanced at Charlotte. She was holding the bat as if ready to use it again. Her face was white and rigid. She stared at Franky-Boy. Almost imperceptibly the leather jacket rose and fell. Franky-Boy was alive. Dougal let out his breath in a long sigh.

The paralysis snapped. He grabbed Miles's bag by its strap. With the other hand he opened the front door. He pushed Charlotte on to the landing. Her eyes remained locked on Franky-Boy. Dougal pulled the door shut. Charlotte stared blankly at the spyhole.

The doors of the three other flats were still closed. The landing and the stairs were quiet. No one was coming to investigate the shot. Not yet. Dougal pushed down the time switch and felt for the keys. Then he remembered. Franky-Boy had taken his set.

'Keys, Charlotte, where are your keys?'

The question broke down her defences. She dropped the bat, which fell with a clatter against the door, and hugged herself. She wrinkled her face as if trying not to cry.

'Keys,' Dougal snapped. '*Now.*'

'The bag,' she whispered.

Dougal crouched and fumbled at the straps. They were already undone. The light went out. He swore. Charlotte switched it on again. He lifted the flap of Miles's bag. Charlotte's perfume wafted out. Inside he glimpsed the wallet of photographs, a large make-up case, a blue file and a video tape. The light glinted on the metal of the keys.

'He's moving,' Charlotte whispered.

A muffled thud penetrated the door, followed by the sound of splintering wood. Dougal thrust a key into the five-lever lock below the Yale. He twisted it and the lock shot smoothly home. Charlotte crouched down and picked up the cricket bat. The handle moved this way and that as though possessed by a devil of its own. The door trembled in its frame. Franky-Boy began to hammer on the wood.

Dougal pulled Charlotte away from the door, and away from the fish-eye lens. He held her against the wall by the switch. She was breathing fast and shallowly. The skin on her arms was warm. She looked so young, Dougal thought: Eleanor's age.

'You left the keys in the lock,' she whispered.

'I had to. He's got mine.'

As if to illustrate the point there was a rattling and scratching on the other side of the door as Franky-Boy tried to insert a key in the blocked keyhole. They heard him swearing.

'Franky-Boy?' Dougal said. 'Franky-Boy?'

Silence fell on the other side of the door.

'Listen,' Dougal went on. 'If you try and knock down the door, the neighbours will hear you. They're very security-conscious round here. And the same goes if you try and shoot your way out. Except in that case you'll probably end up shooting yourself as well.'

The silence continued. Dougal picked up Miles's bag and passed it to Charlotte. He put his mouth near her ear.

'Walk downstairs. Quietly.' He raised his voice again. 'All you need do is wait. Someone's coming, aren't they? They'll let you out. But they won't be pleased if you attract attention, will they? That's the last thing they want. They wouldn't like that at all.'

Charlotte glanced back at the head of the stairs. She slipped silently downwards. The light went out again. Dougal ran after her. She switched on the light at the next landing.

She was waiting for him at the head of the next flight of stairs. 'He's bloody mad,' she hissed. 'I can't believe it. He's got a *gun*.'

'Come on.'

He took the bat and hustled her down the next flight of stairs to the ground floor.

'But what about the police?' Charlotte said. 'You'll have to tell them about me.'

They passed the door of number three. There was a fusillade of shots. Inspector Coleford despised the use of firearms but his opponents had no such qualms.

'We're not going to the police,' Dougal said. 'Don't worry. I'll—'

He stopped suddenly, and grabbed her arm just as she was about to burst through the swing-doors. He pulled her back. The doors had glass panels. From the darkened hall, you could see down the path to the car park, which was lit by security lights. One of the cars had a familiar silhouette like a partly squashed tin can. A bearded man was leaning against the bonnet and smoking a cigarette. Vane was doing the driving.

'What do you mean?' Charlotte demanded. 'That guy had a *gun*. He could have killed us. We can't just let—'

'See the Austin Princess?' Dougal interrupted. 'Third car from the left with the man beside it? He's a friend of the one upstairs.'

As he spoke a dark-coloured Daimler nosed into the access road. Georgie? The car didn't suit him, but it suited Austerford Hall. Vane straightened up and threw away his cigarette.

Charlotte said calmly, 'There's a back entrance to the street behind. You know, where the dustbins go.'

'I don't know. Show me.'

'What about your car?' She was watching the Daimler.

'It's somewhere else. Come on – that may be their boss arriving.'

She led him through a fire door, across a yard packed with bins and out into a back street. She slung Miles's bag over her shoulder. Dougal carried the bat. It was an incongruous object in this setting, but a very reassuring one. It had made a good weapon. You could break bones with a cricket bat. You could kill someone.

Soon they were among people, moving cars and bright lights. The further they got from the flats, the more confident Charlotte became. She walked with a swing; she glanced in shop windows; she attracted interested glances from several youths, and Dougal suspected she was enjoying the attention. He envied her resilience.

'Who was he then?' she said suddenly. 'The big ape in there.'

'I don't know.'

'What was he doing? Looking for you?'

'Looking for Miles, I think.' He hesitated. 'Maybe that's why Miles had to disappear.'

'But why? And why didn't Miles tell me?'

'I don't know,' Dougal said. 'That's one reason why we're not going to the police. It could make things worse for Miles. Anyway, I couldn't tell the police without bringing you into it.'

She nodded as if this made perfect sense to her – as it probably did; you could usually rely on people's self-interest to blind them to the wider implications. They walked on in silence. Charlotte's eyes roved to and fro.

They reached the car park and climbed the steps to the level where he had left the Sierra.

Dougal said, 'Is anything of yours still at the flat?'

Instantly her face filled with fear. 'No. Not now.'

'Sure? Nothing like the photos? Letters?'

She shook her head. 'We're always very careful.'

Careful? It was not the word Dougal would have used. They left the stairs. At this level the car park was almost empty. Human beings seemed very vulnerable in this place of concrete, oil streaks and silence. Dougal held on to the bat as though it were a talisman as well as a weapon. He was very tired. He was desperate to be alone and somewhere safe.

They didn't talk as the car rolled down the ramp. Dougal paid the attendant and drove up to the roundabout. Without being asked, Charlotte gave him directions. She lived in

Sunbury, several miles to the south-west of Richmond. He turned left into a long, wide road with far too many roundabouts. The smell of her perfume was very strong. He rolled down his window a few inches.

'How did you manage with the debate?' he asked.

'Said I wasn't feeling well. I—' She broke off. Dougal heard her breathing accelerating. 'How do you know about that?'

'Because I saw your uncle and Celia on my way to Richmond.'

'Hugo . . .' There was no mistaking the distaste in her voice. But there was something else, something Dougal couldn't identify.

'There was a bomb alert in town,' Dougal went on. 'He was worried about not being able to collect you. How were you going to handle that?'

'One of my friends was going to say I'd gone home early.' She leaned towards him to see the clock in the dashboard. 'Shit, it's later than I thought.'

'When I saw him he was planning to phone the school and ask them to get you a taxi.'

'I don't think anyone would answer. Only the hall was open. The office was locked.'

Dougal thought for a moment. He said, 'So in that case, he'd phone a minicab company and get them to meet you?'

He heard her moving impatiently in her seat. 'Maybe.'

'You don't seem very worried.'

'I'm not. I'll just tell him I stopped off at a friend's house. Because I didn't feel well. That's what I was going to do in any case.'

'He'll believe you?'

'Don't worry. I can handle Hugo. I'll say it was my period and that'll shut him up. He gets all embarrassed. As long as I get home before eleven it won't matter too much. My mum won't get back before then.'

Dougal negotiated another roundabout. *I can handle Hugo.* The casual assumption of power filled him with dread. A much older man besotted with his niece in a manner which everyone assumed was quasi-paternal; no one ever mentioned Charlotte's father. And a young girl with a mature body and a taste for older boyfriends. An acquired taste?

'I can make him do almost anything,' Charlotte said with quiet satisfaction. 'I've always been able to.'

He glanced at her. Her face revealed nothing. Maybe he was inventing problems where none existed. Children could be emotionally ruthless. A lonely middle-aged man could be foolishly sentimental. Sex needn't come into it. Above all, age had nothing to do with the ability of a stronger personality to hold a weaker one in thrall. He remembered the photographs. Perhaps Charlotte had repeated the pattern, albeit with the addition of sex, with another willing victim.

'How did it start with Miles?' he said sharply.

She didn't reply. He let the silence lengthen. His irritation expanded like a balloon, and then the balloon burst.

'I don't give a damn about what you two have been getting up to,' Dougal snapped. 'I'm trying to find Miles.' That was true in a sense which had taken Dougal by surprise; it was also vital to act as though it were literally true. 'His relationship with you made' – Damn: wrong tense – 'makes him vulnerable. Right?'

'How?'

'Vulnerable to blackmail. So it's just possible it has something to do with his disappearance.'

A sniff. 'It started at the BPC Christmas party. You were there, weren't you? Hey, are you a friend of Miles's?'

'Yes. In a way.'

'Really? He never—'

'What happened at the party?'

She giggled unexpectedly. 'Poor old Hugo got salmonella. You remember? He was in such a state. Spent all the time in the toilet, and they had to get an ambulance . . . And what really worried him was how I was going to get home. Miles said he'd take me, because he was coming this way.' A streetlamp showed her face: she was smiling. 'It sort of went on from there. Oh God I wish I knew what's happened to him.'

The tears returned. Dougal let her cry for a couple of miles. Her malice was childish but her grief was adult. She found a tissue in Miles's briefcase and blew her nose violently.

'Do you really think someone knew?' she said.

'Could they have done?'

'That car – I think I've seen it before.'

'The Austin Princess?'

'No – the black one that was coming in.'

'The Daimler?'

'Is that what it is? Listen, I was at the flat last Thursday evening. Miles saw that car in the car park. I think it was the same one. And he went crazy. He wanted me to go but then the bell rang and it was too late. I had to hide in the bedroom instead.'

'Why did he have to answer the door?'

'We had music on – it was obvious someone was in. Anyway he said it was business, it was urgent. I had to sneak out once he'd got the man in the living room.'

'A man?'

'Yeah. I think so. I think Miles called him "he". Is this important?'

'Could be. I don't know. When did you last see him?'

'Saturday evening, at the flat. You go right here, then left at the lights. Is Miles's mum paying you to look for him?'

'Yes.'

'Do you know what I call her? The bitch-witch. Miles hates her.' She looked at Dougal, who said nothing. 'All right, that's not quite true,' she went on. 'But I hate her. She's always getting Miles to go and see her. She's always ringing up when I'm there. And spoiling things. It's not normal, is it, a mother acting like that? And I get so little time with Miles.'

Dougal said. 'Where now?'

'Over there. Then left. You don't approve, do you?'

'It's nothing to do with me,' Dougal said.

'It's my life.'

'So be careful with it. You've only got one.'

They drove in silence for a moment. He guessed his reaction

had confused her: she could have coped with either disapproval or support. She wasn't accustomed to indifference.

They were moving through a mainly residential area – pre-war semi-detached houses and bungalows, a place of pebbledash and satellite dishes and net curtains; there were dozens of almost identical suburbs within commuting distance of London and many other cities.

'It's the next road on the right,' she said, leaning across to look at the clock again. For an instant her arm touched his leg. 'God, it's nearly ten to eleven.'

Dougal pulled into the kerb and stopped, leaving the engine running. He stared through the windscreen. Four youths turned into the road where Charlotte lived. They were playing catch with cans of lager and urging one another on with wordless cries. He heard their shouting diminishing in volume as they moved further away.

'Do you want to take your things out of Miles's bag?' he asked.

'Can't I keep the bag till he comes back?'

'People are asking questions about it. Including Uncle Hugo.'

She lifted the bag on to her lap and took out the make-up case. 'I'll leave the video tape, shall I?'

'Should you?'

'I recorded it on Monday. But it's for Miles – he asked me to. There's something wrong with his timer.'

'*Inspector Coleford*?'

'How did you know?'

Because in the last few days Dougal hadn't been able to avoid him. As tenacious as a shadow, the man was constantly insinuating himself into places where he wasn't wanted.

'I didn't know,' Dougal said. 'I guessed.'

'Could you leave it at the flat for him? Or—' Her voice faltered as she remembered whom they had left there. 'Or at the office. It's the last in the series, it's really good.' She was speaking more and more quickly, perhaps trying to talk herself away from the memory of Franky-Boy.

Dougal put the car into gear and pulled away from the kerb.

'Door to door service, is it?' She leaned towards him and laughed. 'Is that a good idea?'

He turned into her road. The youths were doing something unpleasant to the aerial of a parked BMW. They looked up at the sound of his engine and drifted onwards. As the Sierra passed them, one of them shouted something.

Charlotte's house was about fifty yards up and on the same side of the road. He recognized Hugo Brassard's Rover outside. He pulled up across the driveway of the house beyond it.

'What will you say?' he asked.

'I told you: I left early and went home with a friend, because I didn't feel well. And her dad gave me a lift home. OK?'

'Why didn't you phone?'

'They're not on the phone. Don't worry. It's no problem.' She grinned at him through the half-light, secure in her ability to lie her way out of the difficulty. Then the smile faded. 'If there's any news, can you let me know? Please.'

'I'll do my best,' Dougal said.

'Thanks. For everything.'

Charlotte scrambled out of the car and slammed the door without a backward glance at Dougal.

'Hello, darling,' shouted one of the youths.

She turned towards them and raised her chin. For an instant she held the pose. There was a wolf whistle.

'Give us a kiss,' another voice called.

She turned and ran towards the house. A curtain twitched in the bay window by the front door and Dougal glimpsed Brassard's long, anxious face. The car seemed full of Charlotte's perfume. He wound down the window as far as it would go, let out the clutch and drove away.

15

On Thursday morning Dougal dozed for what seemed like hours as the studio grew brighter and brighter. He was determined to sleep for as long as he could. The camp bed made movement difficult and contributed to the aches in his body; but this was a small price to pay for the absence of bedbugs. It was true that the bites were still itching, but they were no longer so savage.

As he dozed he dreamed. In the dream he was pursuing a woman in a blue dress through central London. He was chasing her because only he could save her from an undefined menace. The streets of Mayfair and Soho were familiar but in the dream something had happened to them. London had become a Third World city overnight. Bombs had torn ragged holes in terraces; windows were shattered, and glass crunched under his feet; gangs of beggars roamed the pavements and looted shops; there was little traffic, and most of it was military. None of this mattered.

The only thing that mattered was whether or not he could save the woman in the blue dress. His anxiety pushed everything else into second place, even fears for his own safety. Occasionally he glimpsed her face. Sometimes it was Celia's. Sometimes it was Charlotte's – not Charlotte as she was now, but Charlotte as she would be in five or ten years' time. Once the woman glanced back, and the face belonged to Miles; that was when Dougal screamed.

'Do you take notice of your dreams?' Mrs Provender had asked.

'Not very often.'

'You should. I find they tell you things . . .'

He dipped in and out of sleep, in and out of the dream. The waking periods grew longer. He thought it was probably mid-morning by now. His watch was in his trouser pocket. The phone was off the hook and buried in cushions. Lying in bed was not particularly comfortable – either physically or mentally – but he was determined to try to enjoy it for as long as possible. He deserved the break.

In the end a bursting bladder and a craving for tea forced him out of bed. The air was still cool, but it was going to be another hot day. Miles's leather bag sat beside the Christmas cactus on the double mattress reserved for bedbugs. The bag and the cactus and the mattress reminded Dougal of all the problems that needed sorting out. He resolutely pushed them to the back of his mind.

He shaved and showered. He had a bruise where Franky-Boy had hit him, but his hair concealed it. The worst visible damage was due to his collision with the table in Miles's hall: below his right eye the skin was dark purple; but the cut had scabbed over and it was smaller than he remembered. There was another bruise on his ribcage. Bending down was painful.

He dressed in clean clothes that miraculously spilled out of the first black plastic sack he investigated. The clean clothes seemed an omen: today marked the point where his luck changed for the better. He made a pot of tea and drank a mug while reading the first two chapters of the latest Barbara Vine novel. This, he told himself firmly, was the life. It was a pity he found it so difficult to concentrate.

He poured himself some more tea and found his watch. It was only twenty past seven. His leisurely morning had been a figment of his imagination, which meant that his show of inde-pendence had been wasted; he felt cheated. Nevertheless there were still grounds for celebration. If Hanbury had been telling the truth about the police investigation, Miles Provender was now safely in the past, no more than a bad memory. And Dougal had paid his debt to Hanbury.

Georgie Sutcombe had approximately twelve hours before

his deadline expired. But that was Hanbury's affair now; it had nothing to do with Dougal. He glanced at Miles's bag. There were other problems. Eleanor was at the head of the list. Margaret Prentisse's words repeated themselves in his memory: *She thinks your silly squabbles are all her fault.* He got up and retrieved the phone from its nest of cushions. He punched in the Kew number. Celia answered on the second ring.

'It's William.'

'What do you want?'

Her voice was an irritable mumble. He guessed he had interrupted her in the middle of breakfast. He decided that an indirect approach might produce better results.

'I found that file. The Custodemus one.'

'Oh good. Where was it?'

'In Miles's briefcase. As you thought.'

'Why didn't you see it before?'

'It was in the wardrobe,' Dougal lied. 'James searched that, not me.'

'Can I come over and collect it?'

'I'll drop it off at your office.' He didn't want her to come here again. 'I've got to get to work early.'

'Whatever suits you best. I'm leaving here in about five minutes.' She added, grudgingly: 'Thanks.'

Celia put down the phone before he had a chance to mention Eleanor, his main reason for phoning. Maybe that was no bad thing. The subject was potentially explosive; it would be better to talk face to face.

While he was finishing his tea he went through Miles's bag. Apart from the slim Custodemus file and Charlotte's video tape there was nothing but a calculator and a wad of paper handkerchiefs. On impulse he opened the file. It contained brief records of Miles's meetings with Hanbury, seven in all. The notes had obviously been compiled either at the time or just afterwards. Some were typed, some were handwritten. He had noted topics discussed and decisions reached. The last meeting had been exactly a week ago, on Thursday.

'NB 1. Raise national awareness,' Miles had written. '2. Local Radio Campaign – case histories. 3. Mailshots(?). 4. PR leads from existing clients.'

There was nothing personal about the notes except indirectly: they showed that Miles had been methodical and indeed painstaking where work was concerned. Dougal had previously assumed Miles to have been a professional cowboy. Now he was forced to revise his opinion yet again. He found the need for these amendments curiously unsettling. It was as if Miles wouldn't stay dead, as if he were conducting a series of rearguard arguments from beyond the grave. And there was something else about the contents of this file, something that worked its way into Dougal's mind as an invisible piece of grit works into an engine. He knew it was there but he couldn't identify it.

Dougal put on a sturdier pair of shoes than those he had worn yesterday and slipped the Barbara Vine novel into his pocket. He decided to walk down to Turnham Green. There was little point in taking the car. At this time of day walking was a pleasure, and the exercise might be good for his ribs. Custodemus's headquarters was near the Strand. He could catch a tube at Turnham Green which would take him almost to the door.

Celia's Volvo was already in the office car park. So, unfortunately, was Brassard's Rover. Dougal didn't want to talk about Eleanor when Hugo Brassard was around. And there was another consideration. He was almost sure that Charlotte wouldn't have been honest with her uncle, and that Brassard wouldn't have been able to recognize the Sierra last night. But the element of doubt was uncomfortable.

He went upstairs. The door was open. The post lay unopened on the reception desk. Dougal hesitated. Celia and Brassard were standing with their backs to him in the main office.

'I shall just put it to her,' Brassard was saying. 'Man to man. I mean face to face. I shall be absolutely frank. Morally she's under an obligation.'

'Don't be ridiculous,' Celia snapped. 'Of course she isn't. It'll just get her back up if you say that.'

'We have to face facts,' Brassard said. 'We have to be sensible.'

'Sensible? I'd—'

Dougal cleared his throat. They turned to look at him. Both were tight-mouthed and frowning, their anger temporarily united and directed towards the interruption. Brassard's complexion was even sallower than usual, and there were spots of dried blood on his neck where he had nicked himself while shaving. Celia looked immaculate but very tired.

Dougal held out the file to her. She came forward to take it. He saw her expression change. He read surprise there, followed by something that might have been anxiety. Perhaps that was wishful thinking.

'What have you done to yourself?' she asked.

'I fell over a table.'

She thought he was lying. She glanced at Brassard, then back to Dougal. 'Do you want some coffee?'

'No thanks.'

Brassard was still frowning. 'No news about Miles, I suppose?'

Dougal shook his head.

'I must say I'm a little surprised.' Brassard stuck his chin out. 'Nothing in his briefcase?'

'Nothing worth mentioning.'

'I thought Custodemus was meant to be pulling out all the stops.'

'We are,' Dougal said.

'But he can't have just vanished. I refuse to believe he's left no trace whatsoever.'

'I'm sure they're doing everything they can,' Celia said.

Simultaneously Dougal asked, 'Then what do you suggest, Hugo? Call in the psychics?'

Brassard's eyebrows shot up. 'Don't be stupid.'

'We've done everything else. Perhaps you'd like to take over the investigation. Or perhaps you'd like to pay for it.'

'Stop it,' Celia said. 'Just stop it, both of you. This isn't helping anyone.'

Brassard scratched one of his shaving cuts, which began to bleed again. 'What about the neighbours?' he asked with the air of a conjurer producing an exceptionally large rabbit from a hat. 'Eh? They might well have seen something.'

'I talked to most of them last night,' Dougal said. 'I could only find two who even know what Miles looks like. It's that sort of place.'

He glanced at Celia, wondering which of them Miles's neighbour had seen on the stairs – Celia or Charlotte. A phone call to the elderly youth would soon settle the point. On the whole Dougal preferred not to know. He had little doubt that Miles had been entangled with both of them, though perhaps for different reasons. The idea that Miles had been two-timing Celia made Dougal furious. It was not a rational response. Loving someone was not a rational business.

'Oh well,' Brassard said. 'Just an idea.'

Dougal half turned, cutting Brassard out of the conversation. 'I rang Margaret last night,' he said to Celia. 'We need to talk about Eleanor. How about this evening?'

Her eyes widened. 'What's wrong?'

'She's not very happy.'

'All right.'

Brassard edged round a desk and outflanked Dougal. 'You haven't forgotten that we're—?'

'I haven't forgotten anything,' Celia said to him. She turned back to Dougal. 'But it's going to be a busy day and possibly a busy evening. I don't know when I'll be free. I'll try and phone you at Custodemus this afternoon.'

He nodded. 'Leave a message with the switchboard if I'm out.'

He looked at her, and she looked back. Brassard was twittering in the background. There were too many emotions, all pulling in different directions. Dougal turned on his heel and walked out of the office.

★　★　★

Dougal strolled into the palm-fringed foyer of Custodemus House. He was carrying a bacon sandwich, a special treat, in a paper bag and his taste-buds were salivating vigorously. The guard on the desk beckoned him over.

'It's your lucky day,' he murmured. 'Mr Hanbury wants you, pronto.'

'He's early.'

'He's in a filthy mood, too. What happened to your face?'

'I tripped over a table.'

The guard chuckled. 'Or her husband came back early?'

Dougal held up the sandwich. 'I've just remembered something. I won't be a moment.'

'I haven't seen you,' the guard said. 'You're a mirage.'

Dougal went back outside, leaned against the wall and munched his sandwich. Five minutes later he returned to the foyer and took the lift to the top floor. Hanbury's secretary was in the outer office. She stared at his face but decided not to comment.

'You're to go straight in,' she said.

Hanbury was at his desk. In front of him were the morning's newspapers. He was smoking and drinking coffee. He stared at Dougal but said nothing until the door was shut.

'That looks nasty.'

'It feels it too.'

Hanbury let it go for the moment. 'The money hasn't been transferred yet. You got through to him all right?'

Dougal nodded. He sat down without waiting to be asked.

'How did he take it?'

'He didn't seem very worried,' Dougal said. 'In fact he laughed at me.'

'There's nothing he can do about it.'

'At the time he may have thought there was.'

'Eh? What do you mean?'

'You know he thinks I'm Miles? He traced Miles's address.'

'How?'

'The shop where Miles bought the camera was in Richmond. Richmond was actually mentioned on the credit-card slip. Miles is in the phone book. All Georgie had to do was phone Directory Enquiries. At least that's what I assume he did.'

Hanbury stubbed out his cigarette. 'You were going to take the camera back and talk to the neighbours. Are you trying to tell me you walked slap-bang into Georgie?'

'Into Franky-Boy. He had a gun.'

Hanbury sat back, rubbing his hands together. 'And?'

'Franky-Boy phoned Georgie to give him the good news. Georgie came over but I left before he arrived. Does he drive a black Daimler?'

Hanbury opened a drawer and took out a buff folder. He turned over a couple of pages and then looked up. 'Navy blue, to be precise. It's registered to Mrs Sutcombe.'

'And I think Vane was there too. Waiting outside with another car, probably Franky-Boy's. An Austin Princess. Was he really a policeman?'

Hanbury glanced at the file. 'Until he was – ah – persuaded to retire a couple of years ago. I understand his tactics as an interrogator were a little unorthodox. His wife divorced him around the same time. How did you get away from Franky-Boy?'

'I hit him with Miles's cricket bat.'

'How very enterprising.'

'He's got my set of flat keys, by the way. And the hall's in a bit of a mess.'

'Indeed . . . So they turned out in force. No wonder Georgie laughed at you. Why didn't you phone me afterwards?'

'Because you didn't give me the number of Joan's flat.'

Hanbury grunted, accepting the point. He got up and strolled to the window. Like the Putney flat, his office had a view of the river.

'You'll have to do something about the hall,' Dougal said softly. 'And perhaps the rest of the flat too. The telephone table got smashed. There's a bit of blood on the carpet.'

'Whose?'

'Mine.' Dougal touched his cheek. 'And also there's a bullet somewhere.'

'Dear me. There were no witnesses, I hope?'

Dougal shook his head.

'Splendid.'

'But they still think I'm Miles,' Dougal said. 'And I wish to God they didn't.'

As he was speaking, one of the phones started to ring. Hanbury frowned and picked it up. He sat down behind the desk. Dougal stared at the ceiling. He thought he recognized the secretary's voice.

'Yes,' Hanbury said. 'No, you were quite right. Leave it with me.' He put down the phone and looked across the desk at Dougal. 'I've got a little job for you this morning.'

'I want some time off,' Dougal said. 'A few days, maybe a week. I need to collect Eleanor.'

'Of course you do, William. And you shall have it. But first things first, eh? This won't take you long.'

You could tell that the village of Thricehurst attracted a nice class of commuter. The platforms of its little railway station were lined with hanging baskets laden with Busy Lizzies, pansies, ivy and several varieties of fuchsia and trailing lobelia. The woodwork and the Victorian cast iron looked freshly painted. The rubbish bin by the exit was empty, and that had been freshly painted too.

The train rattled away towards the south coast. Dougal walked slowly out of the station. It wasn't eleven o'clock but already the heat discouraged exertion.

Thricehurst Station had been tucked discreetly in a hollow more than half a mile from the centre of the old village. Dougal plodded uphill. He passed shops containing beaming butchers and bustling bakers and affluent antique dealers. An off-licence offered twenty-nine types of malt whisky to its discerning customers. He passed tastefully renovated town houses and a tastefully renovated pair of stocks. There was a library, two banks and retail outlets for a number of national chains – all of which were uncharacteristically unobtrusive. Dougal hungered for a few eyesores. He came to a coffee shop that roasted its own beans. The smell made him feel faint with longing. Perhaps Mrs Provender bought her coffee there.

Two teenage girls clip-clopped past on their ponies. Charlotte's age, Dougal thought, but with different tastes. Here was the oldest part of the village – a huddle of cottages, an inn that was now a hotel and the church. Beyond the hotel was the mouth of the Provenders' cul-de-sac.

Outside the Provenders' house he hesitated, nerving himself to go in. A first-floor window shot up.

'Hello! Mr Dougal!' called Clementine Provender. She waved a yellow duster at him. A moment later she opened the front door. She was wearing the dark green slacks and sandals, with a top like a floral poncho. There were smudges of red, swollen skin beneath her eyes. Her lipstick was only partly aligned with her lips.

'Any news?' she said.

'No. I'm sorry.'

She glanced back into the house as if someone had called her. He watched the muscles tightening on her neck. Then she swallowed and turned to face him again.

'I knew there wouldn't be. You would have phoned.' She drew back to let him into the hall and then shut the door behind him. She was having a little difficulty with her articulation. 'But it's good of you to come. What's the state of play?'

Dougal gave her a suitably edited outline of what he and Custodemus had achieved on her behalf. It didn't seem much for her money. She listened, her head inclined towards him, her face intent.

'How are things here?' he asked.

She rubbed her forehead. 'It's been one of those mornings. Carol's ill – that's my daily. I've had to say goodbye to the gardener. And now I've run out of coffee.'

'Are you all right yourself?'

She shrugged. 'The doctor's giving me something. I keep having bad dreams, you see. But I'm coping.'

'Anything I can do?'

'Since you ask, yes.' As she talked she began to drift slowly down the hall; as her legs drifted, so apparently did her mind: 'I'd ask the gardener but of course that's not possible. He's helping the police with their enquiries. Such a silly boy. It seems he got the idea from *Inspector Coleford*. He's not really our gardener, I should add – he only does four hours a week and frankly he's not much good for anything except mowing the lawn and things like that. Where was I?'

'*Inspector Coleford*?'

'Yes – did you see it this week?'

She paused by the open door of the study and glanced into the room. Mr Provender's chair was empty.

'No,' Dougal said. 'But I've got it on video.'

'Me too. A friend lent me it. I never have much luck with the timer on our video. I usually get Miles to do it . . . This week it was all about this man with a pet jaguar. I always thought jaguars were black, but this was spotted, like a leopard. Perhaps it's panthers that are black. Anyway, this one was fed with small boys. It was absolutely terrifying. Super special effects.'

She smiled grimly at Dougal and moved on down the hall. He wondered what the doctor had given her. The voice stumbled on.

'But what really impressed Justin – he's the gardener – was this chap's way of making a living. He used to find houses where the people were out working all day and just pop in and help himself. Justin thought this seemed much better than working so yesterday he gave it a try. It was a house belonging to one of his customers, actually.'

They passed the doorway of the sitting room. Mr Provender wasn't there.

'But unfortunately a neighbour saw him walking out with a video camera under his arm. So now he's helping the police with their enquiries.'

Finally she came to rest in front of a glass-panelled door which opened on to the terrace.

'Yes,' she said, as though answering a question he hadn't asked. 'And someone's coming to see me just before lunch. I'll have to offer them coffee, though it'll delay lunch. Stanley doesn't like waiting for his meals.'

'You need to go out?' Dougal said.

'Yes – there's the coffee, you see. You'll stay for a cup, won't you? And I need to collect a prescription for Stanley and go to the butcher's—'

'Would you like me to stay with Mr Provender?'

'Usually I'd ask Carol, or even Justin. Which was why I was explaining about . . . Would you mind? I'd only be a few minutes.'

'Of course I wouldn't mind.'

'That's very kind of you.'

She opened the door and led the way on to the terrace. Stanley Provender sat in one of the reclining chairs with an unopened magazine on his lap. His empty pipe was on the table beside his chair. He looked up, saw Dougal and nodded.

'Here's Mr Dougal again, dear. He's going to sit with you while I get a little shopping.'

Mr Provender's eyes swung from Dougal to his wife and then back again. 'Miles,' he said in his manly voice. 'Aargh.'

'No dear – Mr Dougal.' She lowered her voice and said to Dougal, 'He's taken quite a fancy to you. I'd better go.'

Dougal sat down. Mrs Provender left. A moment later he heard the door close. He glanced at his host. Mr Provender sat with his hands folded across his stomach staring down the garden. The heavy chin had been shaved this morning. There were creases in his trousers and his shirt had been ironed. He looked like a captain of industry in well-earned repose. Dougal followed his gaze.

What if anything was he looking at? The church tower? The weeds? The unpruned fruit trees? The grass, which had needed cutting forty-eight hours earlier and now needed cutting even more? Justin's workmanship did not inspire confidence.

A doorbell rang inside the house.

Mr Provender sighed in a gusty manner that made his lips quiver. Frowning, he looked at Dougal. 'Miles . . .'

The doorbell rang again.

'Miles?' Mr Provender wriggled in his chair and the magazine slipped from his lap to the ground. 'Miles?'

'It's all right,' Dougal said. 'Don't worry. I'll go.'

Mr Provender smiled. Dougal got up and went inside. The doorbell rang a third time. There was a distinct possibility that Hugo Brassard was waiting on the doorstep. If it was Brassard, it was also possible that Dougal would lose his temper and say something he would afterwards regret.

He opened the door.

'Hello, Miles old son,' Georgie Sutcombe said. 'Fancy seeing you here.'

16

Georgie planted his foot on the threshold. He was wearing a lightweight summer suit, a striped silk tie and shoes which twinkled with polish. He had a leather document case tucked under his arm. He looked as if he were selling something – life insurance perhaps.

'I want a word with you,' he said. 'Why don't you ask me in?'

Dougal was terrified. His mind turned over but produced nothing except a loud and unproductive noise – rather like an engine revving in neutral. He could think of nothing to say, nothing to do.

'I tried to get hold of you last night,' Georgie went on. 'I wanted a word about this Osmond-MacDonald business. I think you got hold of the wrong end of the stick.'

'Aargh . . .' The sound was faint but desperate.

'Your old man, is it?' Georgie said, edging into the hall. 'Don't look so surprised, Miles.'

'I'm not Miles.'

'Come on. You'll have to do better than that. I know about you, I know about your parents. It's all a matter of research and forward planning. Use your head.'

To emphasize the point, Georgie tapped his own head just above and in front of his left ear. *Tap, tap, tap.* Dougal had used the hammer on Miles's head at precisely the same place. The horror of the memory jolted him, which had the side-effect of ramming his mind into gear.

'Aargh . . .'

Dougal shut the door and walked towards the terrace. Georgie followed.

'Nice little place you've got here,' Georgie said. 'Tasteful – just what I like myself.'

It was obvious what had happened, Dougal thought: Georgie had done some research at Miles's flat.

'I tried to get hold of you at Brassard Prentisse,' Georgie continued. 'They said you weren't in the office. I *was* surprised.'

But the really significant thing, Dougal thought, was that Georgie had dared to come here at all. It was all wrong. Hanbury must have miscalculated.

The door to the terrace was wide open. Dougal went outside. Stanley Provender was leaning forward and gripping the arms of his chair. His face gleamed with sweat.

'It's all right,' Dougal said as calmly as he could. 'This is Mr Sutcombe.'

Mr Provender sighed. The hands relaxed. He sat back in his chair. One hand groped for the pipe. The other patted his lap. A puzzled expression settled on the chalky face.

'Aargh,' Mr Provender said. 'Miles.'

'That's right,' Georgie said. 'Miles. Just what I say.'

Hands in pockets, he strolled across the terrace and put his document case on the table. He stared down at Stanley Provender. He smiled – a smile with genuine warmth – and Mr Provender smiled back. Next, Georgie bent down and picked up the magazine. He put it on Mr Provender's lap. Mr Provender beamed at him, and Georgie beamed back.

'You brainless old turd,' Georgie said pleasantly. 'I think people like you should be exterminated. Would you like that?'

Mr Provender nodded. He put the pipe in his mouth, sucked hard and went on smiling.

'Good,' Georgie said. 'Vermin, that's what you are.'

'What do you want?' Dougal said.

Georgie wasn't taking any risks, even now. He wandered to the edge of the terrace and stared at the overgrown garden. Dougal reluctantly joined him.

'You really are a prick, aren't you?' Georgie said softly. 'If you're going to blackmail someone you want to be sure of your facts. Like I said – research. And also you've got to work out how to handle it if something goes wrong. That's where the forward planning comes in. See?'

He paused, as if expecting Dougal to say something. Dougal said nothing. Silence was a temporary refuge, and he desperately needed time to think. First, Georgie was aware of Stanley Provender's condition, which suggested that he or Vane had done their homework either at the flat or at Thricehurst; but they hadn't done enough homework because they didn't yet know that Miles was missing. Second, it might be more than coincidence that Georgie arrived after Mrs Provender had gone shopping. Perhaps he or one of his employees had been watching the house. It was not impossible that Vane and Franky-Boy were lurking in the wings.

Georgie glanced over his shoulder at Mr Provender, gave him a wave and turned back to Dougal. 'I was in the area anyway – I thought I'd pop in here on the off chance. I could always leave a message with your parents, I thought. But no need. Bull's-eye, eh?'

'You've got about eight hours left,' Dougal said.

'Leave it out, will you?'

'The Osmond-MacDonald material is fully documented,' Dougal heard himself saying in a prim voice he found it hard to believe was his own.

'Most of the old dears are dead. Or half blind. Or else they're like your old man.' He waved again at Mr Provender, who simpered an acknowledgement. 'Not much use in the witness box, eh? Once again, that's forward planning. Take my tip: if you want to defraud someone, go for the elderly. They think slower and die quicker.'

'Someone will remember you.'

'Remember Mr Osmond, you mean. I doubt it. By all accounts he wasn't a fool. He'd have thought of that, don't you think? Personally I'd be very surprised if any of his old clients would recognize him now. Come to think of it, he probably disguised himself when he visited them. Amazing what you can do with a pair of specs and a couple of pads in your mouth.'

'The money from the Osmond-MacDonald account—'

'I don't know if you've tried to trace what happened to that money,' Georgie interrupted. 'If not, let me give you a word of advice: don't waste your time. It all happened years ago. It's ancient history. People have moved on, companies have merged or crashed. You'd have to trace hundreds of transactions in places all around the world; you'd need dozens of names and numbers. Like I said, forward planning: that's the key.'

'You're bluffing,' Dougal said.

'Am I? Use your head, Miles.' Georgie's forefinger went tap, tap, tap. 'Would I be here if I was bluffing? Even if I was, you'd still have to prove I was Osmond.'

'There must be photos—'

'Not to my knowledge.'

'Dental records.'

'Ozzie didn't have a dentist,' Georgie grinned. 'He didn't exist, you see – not outside his work.'

'Fingerprints.'

Georgie held up his hands, the palms towards Dougal and the fingers splayed out. 'Some people have to be very careful what they touch. Allergies and stuff like that. Ozzie said he had a skin disease, a bit like psoriasis. Wore gloves most of the time. Didn't you know?'

'Maybe it's not legally provable,' Dougal began, 'but—'

'Listen, Miles.' Georgie put his head very close to Dougal's. 'I should complain to the police about this. Blackmail's a very serious offence. There's no reason why I shouldn't bring in the boys in blue, is there? It's not as if you can prove anything. Or I could ask Franky-Boy to have a word with your parents instead, and with yourself of course. After last night, he'd rather like that.'

Dougal took a step backwards. He said nothing.

'Or – just possibly – I might let you off with a caution. You'd have to sign something, naturally.' Georgie jerked his head towards the table, towards the document case. 'It's all ready. And I'd want to know your sources.'

Dougal shrugged. *Damn Hanbury.* 'I'm a journalist by training. You hear things.'

Georgie shook his head. 'You can do better than that.'

What happened next took Dougal completely by surprise. Georgie spun round and walked quickly to Mr Provender.

'Arsehole,' he shouted.

Mr Provender's face crumpled, just like Eleanor's did when you shouted at her. And then, just like Eleanor, he began to cry. Dougal heard Mrs Provender's voice in his memory: *Try and keep your voice down. Otherwise the old boy gets upset. Funny, eh? I think someone must have shouted at him a long time ago.*

Georgie snatched the pipe from the old man's mouth. Mr Provender jerked forward and cried out. His hands twitched. Tears ran down the powdery cheeks, zigzagging through a maze of furrows.

'Stop that,' Dougal said. 'Stop it.'

Georgie held the pipe in both hands a few inches away from Mr Provender's face. He smiled and snapped the pipe in two. He lobbed the pieces into a rose bush at the end of the terrace. Mr Provender whimpered.

Dougal grabbed Georgie's right arm. A hand sliced at his wrist. Dougal yelped and let go.

'Aargh,' Mr Provender said, and twisted in his chair as though someone had passed an electric current through him.

'I don't think you heard me, Miles,' Georgie said. 'I want your sources, and I want them now.'

Dougal ignored him. He walked to the end of the terrace. The remains of the pipe had fallen through the branches to the bare earth. A thorn scratched his thumb as he lifted them out. The stem had snapped where it screwed into the bowl.

Georgie picked up the leather document case and clasped it to his chest. 'Who told you all this crap?'

Dougal sucked a bead of blood from his thumb. He gave the pieces of pipe to Mr Provender, who smiled uncertainly at him.

'Miles . . .?' the old man said.

The big, well-shaped hands tried to fit the pieces together again. Dougal turned to Georgie. He knew that whatever happened he mustn't allow himself to show his anger.

'I like to be thorough,' Dougal said. 'I like to do my research. What's your wife going to say about all this?'

Georgie smiled. 'I'll tell her everything. Why not? She'll want me to go to the police, I imagine.'

'Will you tell her about Joan Trotwood?' Dougal asked.

The smile stayed, but only just. 'Who?'

'Your common-law wife. Will you tell Mrs Sutcombe why you were calling yourself Trotwood? Why you had Franky-Boy throw Joan Trotwood off your balcony at the villa? Will you tell her about the way you murdered your unborn child?'

'Now listen—'

'For a while you must have been sleeping with them both. And for a while each of them must have been carrying your child. Will you tell Mrs Sutcombe that?'

'Shut up. It's bullshit.'

'I've talked to the Spanish authorities,' Dougal said. 'And I've got an affidavit from a nurse at the clinic Mrs Trotwood went to. Nothing like research, is there? When I've traced Mrs Trotwood herself, I'm sure she'll be happy to confirm all this. And of course she'll probably want to swap notes with Mrs Sutcombe. Maybe *she'll* want to press charges. Who knows? I wouldn't be surprised if one of the tabloids bought her story. I understand Mrs Trotwood's quite good-looking.'

Georgie's eyes moved – this way and that, from Dougal to Mr Provender, from the ground to the door.

'Mrs Sutcombe still owns Austerford, doesn't she?' Dougal went on, keeping his voice low and even-toned, to avoid upsetting Mr Provender. 'And the baby's due next month. All being well. You must find her high blood pressure very worrying. And the deal with your Japanese friends hasn't been finalized yet. You were lucky to get them to invest in property development. They have to be scrupulous about who they deal with. But of course you know all this.'

'You are a dead man,' Georgie said quietly, pausing between each word and emphasizing the last three, *a – dead – man*, with stabs of his finger: *tap, tap, tap.*

'Four hundred thousand pounds seems quite a small price when you think what it buys you.' Dougal smiled reassuringly at Mr Provender and turned back to Georgie. 'Freedom, wealth and a happy family. You don't deserve any of it.'

'Get fucked.'

They stared at each other. Georgie's lips were so tightly shut that the skin had puckered at the corners.

'Let me show you out,' Dougal said.

Without a backward glance he went into the hall. He heard Georgie following. At the front door Dougal stopped.

'Don't try any short cuts, will you?' he said. 'Like trying to have me killed, or causing problems here. I've left letters. All part of my forward planning.'

He opened the door. Georgie went out. On the doorstep he looked back as if trying to memorize Dougal's face. He let out his breath in an almost silent whistle.

From the cul-de-sac came an amalgam of sounds – rattles and wheezes, with the occasional squeak – growing gradually louder. Dougal and Georgie turned towards the noise. Mrs Provender was hauling a two-wheeled shopping trolley along the pavement towards the house. Her face was pink and her breathing was laboured.

Georgie swore. He walked quickly towards the mouth of the cul-de-sac. Mrs Provender looked up at him as he passed. He ignored her. She was puffing vigorously like a small steam engine climbing a steep hill.

'Who was that?' she said to Dougal.

'He was selling insurance, I think. Something like that.'

'How's the old boy been?'

'He broke his pipe. He was a bit upset. But I think he's more or less OK now. Let me take that.'

Dougal picked up the shopping trolley, lifted it into the house and carried it down the hall to the kitchen. He looked back to see Mrs Provender going on to the terrace. He rested both hands on the kitchen table. He started to shiver. The shivering came in waves. At the peaks of the waves his teeth chattered.

In a trough between the waves he heard Stanley Provender's voice uplifted in song: 'Oh, my darling, oh my darling, oh my darling Clementine . . .'

Slowly the waves subsided. The shaking stopped, at least for the time being.

He filled the kettle and plugged it in. He went back to the terrace. Mrs Provender was sitting by her husband and holding his hand. Mr Provender's eyes were closed, and he held the bowl of his pipe in his free hand. Mrs Provender looked up.

'I'll make some coffee in a moment,' she said. 'Or perhaps a cold drink would be better?'

'Is there anything I can do while I'm here?'

'You've done enough already.'

'I'd like to help.' Dougal looked away from her. 'How about the lawn? I could give it a trim.'

'We couldn't possibly—'

He smiled at her. 'You could, you know.'

The grim face cracked. She smiled back. 'The old boy would like it.'

The sun was high in the sky. Dougal trundled up and down the lawn – not a vast area, but irregularly laid out to give an impression of size. The Provenders had a heavy motor mower with gleaming blades that gobbled up the grass.

Mr Provender watched intently from the terrace. When the pattern of the mowing brought Dougal close to the terrace, Mr Provender would raise his hand a few inches; Dougal would smile and wave back. Repetition made the smile mechanical and meaningless, but Mr Provender did not seem to mind.

It was very hot. After a while Dougal took off his shirt and exposed his pale city skin to the air. The sweat dripped down his face, his neck and his body. Georgie's visit had stirred up the contents of his mind. The work calmed him. His thoughts gradually settled down, some of them in different places from before. Terror had a curious effect on the mind. Afterwards you saw things from a different perspective, as though you'd had a dose of electroconvulsive therapy. You thought of possible answers to questions you'd never asked before. It was all very unsettling.

Mrs Provender came out with a battered straw hat and a glass of iced lemonade. Dougal turned off the mower.

'You don't want sunstroke, do you?' she said. 'And you must keep your fluids up.'

The lemonade was home-made and very good. The hat fitted perfectly.

'It's Miles's, actually – you must have the same size head.'

Oh Christ – if the cap fits, wear it.

'You'll stay to lunch, of course.' She surged on before Dougal had time to protest. 'Don't think I'm prying, but how did you get those bruises? They look quite nasty.'

'I fell over a table,' he said. 'Please don't worry about lunch. What about your visitor?'

'Oh she phoned. Apparently she was delayed at the office, so she's going to be a little late. I think I'd better lay the table for four.'

She?

Dougal finished the lemonade and gave Mrs Provender the glass.

She looked into his face. 'You don't think Miles will come back, do you? Ever. You wouldn't actually say it on the phone yesterday, but that's what you meant.'

'I think—' Dougal stopped, and then tried again. 'Sometimes it's best to assume the worst is true. And go on from there.'

She nodded. 'And if it isn't true, it doesn't matter? And if it is, you're prepared?'

Dougal said nothing.

After a moment, she sighed and said, 'Lunch in about twenty minutes.' She walked back to the house.

Dougal went to empty the grass cuttings on the compost heap. When he came back, Celia was talking to the Provenders on the terrace. Mrs Provender waved him over.

'You two know each other, don't you?'

'Aargh,' said Mr Provender.

Dougal smiled at Celia. 'Oh yes.'

'Hello, William.'

'Aargh,' said Mr Provender, shaking his head judiciously. 'Miles.'

17

After lunch, Celia casually offered Dougal a lift back to London. He accepted. Mrs Provender came outside to wave them off. Dougal rolled down his window and waved back.

'See you next week,' Mrs Provender called.

The Volvo turned out of the cul-de-sac. Dougal couldn't see any midnight-blue Daimlers or black Jaguars. They drove through the village and down the hill towards the station. Celia let the car drift towards the kerb.

'Would you rather go by train?' she asked.

'Not unless you'd like me to.'

'I thought you might just have wanted an excuse to get away.'

'I wanted an excuse to talk to you,' he said.

'About Eleanor?'

'Among other things.'

He glanced at her. She looked a little pinker than usual, but perhaps that was due to the sun. Her eyes were on the road. She was a good driver – smooth, fast and decisive.

They drove on. Soon they were in the open country. The warm air flowed through the open windows. It smelled of tar, exhaust fumes and manure.

'Mrs Provender doesn't want to help you,' Dougal said. 'Is that right?'

Celia nodded.

'Do you mind?'

'Without Miles, there's no point in her investing in us. Besides, there's not much left to invest in. I can't blame her.'

He said nothing. She hadn't answered the question.

A moment later, she went on. 'Before I left the office, we

had three phone calls. One was from the bank, saying they weren't going to wait any longer. Hugo's trying to make them change their mind, but they won't. The next call was from James Hanbury. He was very nice about it all . . . he said in the circumstances he thought Custodemus had better look elsewhere for their PR. And the third one was my mystery man – you remember?'

'The one who made you sign a letter of confidentiality?'

'That's the one. Now he's pulled out too. No reason given. I suppose he'd heard rumours about us. Still it was a bit odd, the whole thing.'

'How come?'

'My secretary was on the switchboard. She said he asked for Miles first. But he doesn't know Miles.'

They drove on. The tree-lined country road came to a roundabout. Celia turned on to a dual carriageway. The car picked up speed. They rolled up their windows.

After another pause, she said, 'By the way, you were quite right.'

'What about?'

'What you said yesterday evening. Remember? You told Hugo and me that we didn't give a damn about the Provenders, that we just wanted their money.'

Dougal didn't answer. His arrogance amazed him. Who was he to judge Celia? Killing Miles was infinitely worse than lusting after his parents' money. Murder was worse than greed, perhaps worse than anything. Not murder, he protested to himself, but an accidental killing while acting in self-defence. Then the horror of it gripped him. He turned his head and stared out of the window so that there was no risk of Celia's seeing his face. He would never know which description was true. Maybe two taps with the hammer had been self-defence: maybe the third had made it murder.

'I wish I knew what was going on in your head,' Celia said. 'You disapprove, don't you?'

He glanced at her. 'Only of myself.'

'Why?'

He shook his head. It was unexpectedly tempting to tell her the truth. But if he did, it would be for the wrong reasons: to help himself not her; perhaps in the hope of an absolution she couldn't give him. Forgiveness on those terms meant asking her to share responsibility for what he had done.

'You're an odd man.'

'I can't change that.'

'No.'

Another silence settled around them, a silence enclosed in a shell of noise from the engine and the rushing air.

'It's been a nightmare, these last few months,' Celia said suddenly. 'I'm sorry.'

'It's all right,' he said. 'Don't worry.'

'Things got out of proportion. You know something? I hope Miles is OK, for his parents' sake. But in a way I'm relieved that we're not going to be Brassard Prentisse Provender after all.'

Dougal was so surprised he let the silence linger too long. 'I thought you liked him,' he said at last.

'I do. And he works hard. But it wouldn't have been the same with him as a full partner. He wanted to change things.'

'I meant I thought you liked him personally.'

The car jerked forward as if Celia's foot had slipped on the accelerator. All she said was, 'I like Hugo too. Personally.'

Dougal blinked. They drove on. Neither of them spoke for several miles.

'What will you do now?' he asked.

'Put the house on the market, try and find somewhere smaller. Maybe try and work from home eventually.'

'Talking of the house,' Dougal said carefully, 'did you ever find that missing set of keys?'

'No. They're probably kicking round the office. I thought they were in my desk. It doesn't matter now.'

Another mile went by.

'What were you going to say about Eleanor?' Celia asked.

'According to Margaret, she's very upset,' Dougal said. 'I'm going to see her this evening.'

'I was thinking of going down there myself.'

'We could go together.'

'Why not? Save petrol. When?'

'I've got a meeting in town. I'm free after that. Shall I meet you at Kew?'

'OK.'

They reached the motorway. Celia pushed the car into the fast lane and put her foot down. They talked about Eleanor.

'Were you thinking of staying the night?' Celia said.

'Yes.'

'Me too. What about your job?'

'I'm taking some leave.'

'You realize that Margaret won't stop telling us what awful parents we are?'

'Maybe she has a point,' Dougal said.

Celia glanced at him and then back at the road. He thought she was looking much more relaxed than he had seen her look for weeks, if not months.

'And if Margaret's right,' Celia said, 'what do you propose we do about it?'

Tea was served in the Mortbank Room of the Royal Commonwealth Institute between half past three and five o'clock. When Dougal arrived, Hanbury was sitting near one of the windows. Hanbury waved him over and asked the waitress to bring them another cup.

'Lapsang,' Hanbury said. 'Nothing like it on a hot afternoon.'

Several other people were drinking tea or reading magazines; but the Mortbank Room was so enormous that there was no risk of being overheard.

'I had a call from Windward Credit just before I left the office,' Hanbury went on. 'The money's come through.'

'Good,' Dougal said, sitting down.

'You've done a marvellous job.' Hanbury glanced at his watch. 'But I'm afraid I can only spare you five minutes. I'm meeting Charlie here.'

'Who?'

'I thought I mentioned him – my minister. We're going to have a chat about the commission. Now what's your problem?'

'It's not just my problem,' Dougal said. 'Georgie came down to Thricehurst. He still thinks I'm Miles. He said I couldn't prove he was Osmond. And then he started getting nasty.'

Hanbury sat up sharply. 'What did you do?'

'Hit him over the head with Joan. I threatened to tell his wife about the whole business.'

'Oh, William. That's the last thing you—'

'What else could I do?' Dougal interrupted. 'I didn't mention you, and I said I hadn't traced Joan yet. He still thinks I was acting off my own bat. And the main thing is, he's paid up.'

The waitress brought another cup. Hanbury automatically flashed a smile at her. He waited until she was out of earshot.

'By and large you seem to have coped very well. Of course we'll make sure there are no repercussions. That's the least I can do.'

He began to pour Dougal's tea.

'There are one or two other things you can do,' Dougal said.

'Oh?'

'I'd like to take some leave. Until Monday week.'

'Of course you shall.' Hanbury passed the cup to Dougal. 'You must be shattered.'

'From then on I'd like to work full time. And I'd like a rise, too.'

Hanbury paused with his own cup halfway to his lips. He raised his eyebrows. 'I'm afraid any form of promotion is out of the question. In the short term, at least. Much as I'd like to—'

'I'm sure you'll manage,' Dougal said. 'You always do.'

'I don't think I understand.' Hanbury looked at his watch again. 'Could we carry on with this another time perhaps?'

'I'd rather get it over with.'

'The Minister—'

'The Minister can wait,' Dougal said. 'I need more money because Brassard Prentisse Communications is folding, partly because people like you have withdrawn their accounts. This means that Celia won't have an income.'

'Terribly sad, but what can one do?' Hanbury spread his hands wide. 'It's this beastly recession.'

'I've told you what you can do,' Dougal said patiently. 'You can give me a substantial rise.'

'William – I hate to remind you of this, but we had an arrangement: you were helping me because I had been able to help you. Remember? Sunday night?'

'Oh I remember all right,' Dougal said. 'My trouble is, I'm too credulous. I believed Miles when he said that Celia had asked him to come. But she didn't. You did.'

'You need a break. Your mind's playing tricks on you. We'll have dinner tonight and talk this through and—'

'Miles was working for you, James. When you turned up on Sunday night, you hadn't come to help me. You'd come to help Miles, hadn't you?'

'Don't be absurd.'

'On Sunday you packed me off to Northampton to keep me out of the way. Then the duty officer told you I was back in London. So you phoned the studio, and there was no answer. You realized I was probably in Kew, and you thought you'd better join the party.'

'Just as well I did, eh?' Hanbury said, smiling. 'You certainly needed a friend.' He lowered his voice. 'I take it you aren't disputing what happened to Miles?'

Dougal shook his head.

'Well then,' Hanbury went on. 'And what about the fact that Celia gave him the keys?'

'He found a spare set in her desk at the office.'

'And full instructions for the burglar alarm no doubt? Aren't you being a little overimaginative? Almost – well, I hate to use the word – almost *paranoid*.'

'The alarm happens to be a Custodemus model. I got it through you at a trade discount. So all you needed to do was pull out the installation report.'

'But the switches are electronic. And they're controlled by individual numbers chosen by the customers.'

'Not in this case. There's only a manual switch. It's all in the engineer's report.'

Hanbury poured himself another cup of tea. 'This is academic.'

'There's nothing academic about four hundred thousand pounds,' Dougal snapped.

'There's no need to tell the whole world about it.'

'You wanted to trace Georgie Sutcombe so you could blackmail him. Hugo and Miles knew about Celia's mystery client. But they didn't know who it was. You knew who, because you'd recommended him to Celia in the first place. But you didn't know how to get hold of him. I expect you got Miles to poke around the office first, probably last Friday. He found the keys, but the Austerford file was——'

'Why Miles, eh? If this twaddle were true, why should I take the risk of involving someone else?'

'Because it's a smaller risk than the risks you'd be taking if you did these things yourself. You used me for the same reason. So next you sent Miles to Kew when you knew the house was empty. Sure enough, Miles found the Austerford file upstairs. He wrote the phone number on a bit of paper . . . I put it on the mantelpiece along with everything else in his pockets. Where you found it.'

Hanbury sighed. 'This is all very well. But why should Miles break the law on my behalf?'

'Because you were blackmailing him.'

'What on earth with?'

'Charlotte.'

Hanbury looked over the rim of his cup at Dougal. 'I beg your pardon?'

'He was having sexual relations with a minor. I think you

183

turned up unexpectedly at his flat on Thursday evening. At first I assumed you'd met him during the day, but it must have been the evening. And I know it was Thursday because Miles dated the notes he made. According to Brassard, Miles went down to Bournemouth on Thursday.'

'A mistake. Hugo's in such a state he doesn't know if he's coming or going.'

'But he showed us Miles's diary. Remember? There was no record of an appointment in there. And there's another thing. You implied you'd never been to Miles's flat before we searched it. But you had. You knew your way around – which door was which, and so on.'

'Merely an educated guess. After all—'

'It won't work, James.' Dougal knew it was time to follow Inspector Coleford's example: when in doubt, bluff. 'Charlotte saw your car. And you saw Charlotte.'

Hanbury shook his head, as if to convey that the accusation was too ridiculous to be worth the trouble of rebutting. Dougal waited. It was all down to Inspector Coleford and the jaguar. At night all cats are grey. In the evening a black Jaguar can look much the same as a navy-blue Daimler, especially when seen at a distance by someone who knows little about cars.

Dougal picked up his cup. 'And of course that's why you pretended that Charlotte's perfume was Miles's aftershave.'

There was a long pause. Dougal drank his tea.

'Ah – you have been busy,' Hanbury said. 'Of course appearances can be very misleading.'

'Yes, indeed. Had you lined up the Ford Escort in Slough right from the start? Because Miles could link you with Georgie, so he was better out of the way? Was he threatening to make trouble?'

'Don't be so machiavellian, William.'

'It's not me who's being machiavellian,' Dougal pointed out. 'I leave that to you.'

Hanbury looked at his watch for the third time. 'I should be downstairs. This is quite unprovable, you know.'

'Of course it's unprovable. But I don't have to prove it, do I?'

'You mean you're contemplating sending a libellous postcard to Austerford Hall? Something of that nature?'

Dougal shrugged. 'At present Georgie doesn't even suspect that you and Joan are involved. I imagine you'd like it to stay that way. So would I.'

Hanbury examined his hands, first one side and then the other, as if checking that they were perfectly clean. Then he looked at Dougal. His plump, smooth face broke into a smile.

'What a sense of humour you've got.'

'James, it's—'

Hanbury held up a hand. 'As it happens, I've been considering appointing a confidential personal assistant. In view of – ah – your circumstances I might be able to bring the appointment forward. On compassionate grounds.'

'To Monday week,' Dougal suggested.

'Ah – well, why not?'

'Shall we say double my present salary as I'll be working full time?'

'All right. But you'll earn it, believe me. This won't be a sinecure.'

'In that case you may want to add a small token of appreciation in advance. Let's make it five thousand a year.'

Unexpectedly Hanbury chuckled. 'You know what I like about you, William? You're always so reasonable. Very well.'

'Thank you.'

'Don't thank me. It's a pleasure. That's what friends are for, eh?'

A porter came into the room. He looked around, saw Hanbury and came over to them. He bent down and murmured something in Hanbury's ear. Hanbury nodded and got up.

'The Minister's here. Will you excuse me?'

'Of course,' Dougal said.

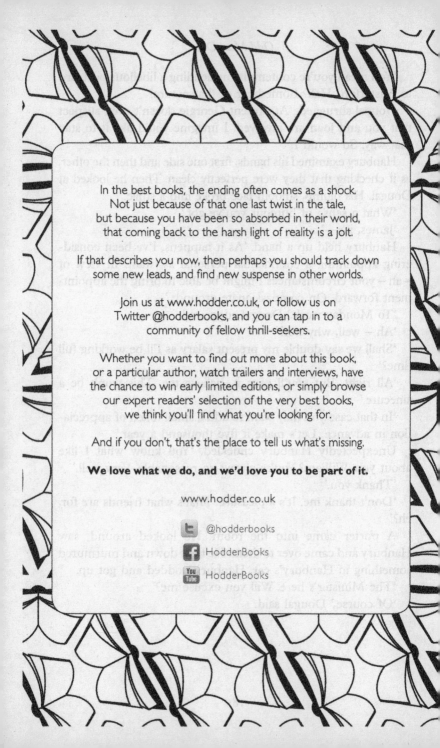